Meg stopped halfway up the path, her heart pounding. She didn't understand it, but something about the tall, handsome man with the iron-gray hair—her adversary, Evan Alton—undid her.

Any other impressions she got were short-circuited on their way to her brain by the cries of what sounded like a dozen babies. She followed the wails to a sprawling sitting room and discovered a sight more startling than walking in on all that howling. Evan Alton sat in a rocker with a twin on each shoulder, attempting to burp both babies at the same time.

"Well, this is a photo op the local newspaper would probably kill for," Meg drawled. "The great and powerful Evan Alton brought low by fourteen pounds of newborn."

Books by Kate Welsh

Love Inspired

KATE WELSH

is a two-time winner of Romance Writers of America's coveted Golden Heart® and a finalist for RWA's RITA® Award in 1999. Kate lives in Havertown, Pennsylvania, with her husband of over thirty years. When not at work in her home-office, creating stories and the characters that populate them, Kate fills her time in other creative outlets. There are few crafts she hasn't tried at least once or a sewing project that hasn't been a delicious temptation. Those ideas she can't resist grace her home or those of friends and family.

As a child she often lost herself in creating make-believe worlds and happily-ever-after tales. Kate turned back to creating happy endings when her husband challenged her to write down the stories in her head. With Jesus so much a part of her life, Kate found it natural to incorporate Him in her writing. Her goal is to entertain her readers with wholesome stories of the love between two people the Lord has brought together and to teach His truths while she entertains.

AUTUMN PROMISES

KATE WELSH

Published by Steeple Hill Books™

STEEPLE HILL BOOKS

Steeple
Hill®

ISBN 0-373-87275-5

AUTUMN PROMISES

Copyright © 2004 by Kate Welsh

www.SteepleHill.com

Printed in U.S.A.

Trust in the LORD with all your heart,
And lean not on your own understanding.
In all your ways acknowledge Him,
And He shall direct your paths.

—Proverbs 3:5-6

To Patience Smith. Thanks so much for all your years of support and for being such a great sounding board over the years.

Prologue

The phone on Meg Taggert's bedside table pealed in the night. She sat up, instantly awake, and snatched it up. She knew who it was—and what it was about!

"So, I'm a grandmother," she said before the person on the other end had a chance to say a word.

A deep chuckle from her son, Jack, reverberated over the wires. "Been given the gift of prophecy since Beth and I moved to Colorado?"

She smiled to herself, but took a tone of pretended offense. "Don't be difficult, Jackson Wade Alton. I'm a grandmother now—therefore, I deserve a certain amount of delicate treatment."

"Who are you trying to kid? You're as tough as old boots, Mom, even if you are a hundred times prettier. But I'm too tired to keep you in suspense.

You have a grandson and a granddaughter and every-one is fine. But everything didn't go so well for a while. Beth had to have a C-section. The doctors got worried about signs of fetal distress.''

And she'd thought she was awake before! ''But they're all fine now?''

''They're incredible. Beth was the most incredible of all. I nearly fainted when the OB said C-section. All Beth said was, 'Then let's get it done. I want to hold my babies.' I love her so much, Mom.'' Jack's voice showed his strain. ''I never prayed so hard in my life. I'm beginning to understand what Dad felt all those years ago when Mama died.''

She refused to discuss the arrogant man who had adopted her precious son as a newborn. ''Are you finally going to tell me what these extraordinary grandchildren of mine are named?''

''Maggie Anne after Beth's nanny and Wade Jack-son after my biological father. Six pounds each and nineteen inches long.''

Meg closed her eyes, fighting tears and picturing the handsome face of Jack's father—her long dead fiancé. Finally someone would bear his name. ''Oh, that's wonderful,'' she whispered, choked up and not doing a very good job of hiding it. She cleared her throat. ''And what does your father think of the names?''

''He wanted Maggie to be called Martha after Mama, but Maggie O'Neill raised Beth. She might as well have been Beth's mother for all the affection she ever got from her own mother. With Maggie so recently gone, I couldn't ask Beth to name our daughter anything else. She has a right to name one of the babies, so we split the honor down gender lines. Besides, it's close to your name, too. Of course, I also think Dad's hurt about Wade's name, but I had to do this. He and Mama should have named me the way you asked when they adopted me.''

Meg held her tongue. She refused to tarnish this moment with contention and what she thought of Evan Alton and his failures as a father. Nothing could excuse those failures, considering that he'd failed when she'd entrusted him with her precious child, her only link to the man she still loved with all her heart. Wade might have died in the jungles of Vietnam, but he lived in her heart and dreams still. She understood how Evan could still grieve for his long-dead wife, but she didn't understand how he could have allowed that grief to overshadow his relationship with his children.

She reminded herself that she had no right to hold a grudge when Jack didn't, and that the Lord had, as usual, used bad happenings for good. Had Evan not had such a poor relationship with Jack, her son would never have gone in search of his biological mother and she wouldn't have her son, her daughter-in-law and now two grandchildren to love.

Oh, she couldn't wait to visit the Circle A and get her hands on those precious babies.

Chapter One

Evan looked up from his granddaughter Maggie's sweet newborn face when his son, Jackson, walked into the living room. Jackson had his fretting son on his shoulder, patting the infant on his back.

"Wade doesn't look to be too happy today," Evan said. "And neither do you, son. Problem?"

Jackson's eyebrows dipped as his frown deepened. "Beth's running a fever. Doc wants to see her. She's not up to driving into town, and I don't want her to go alone in any case. I'm worried, Dad. I guess Wade picked up on my mood."

Maggie started to fuss, so Evan transferred her to his shoulder. "Try not to worry, son. Beth's strong. I'm sure it's nothing serious."

Jackson grimaced. "Beth and I have been so happy these last two years. I have a bad feeling about it.

Like that's all about to change. I know I was young, but I remember the way Mama never seemed to spring back after Crystal's birth. And no one in child-birth classes said anything about spiking high fevers a week after delivery.''

"Don't harbor worries about history repeating it-self. That's a bunch of nonsense," Evan told Jackson, but he felt his spirits dip as memories of those last two years with Martha rolled over him. He'd watched helplessly as the cancer took her from him, one cell at a time.

Jackson nodded, but he didn't look convinced. "If you don't have other plans, do you think you could give Anna a hand with the twins while we're gone? Seth has the ranch work handled for me, but I hate to impose on Anna. She's a housekeeper, not a baby-sitter.''

"Anna's crazy about the twins. Don't worry about her. And don't forget about me. There's nothing I'd rather do than help with them," Evan replied. He wished Jackson didn't look so surprised by that. Which was his own fault, not his son's, of course. But it hurt knowing he'd put that disbelief into Jack-son's eyes all by himself. For too many years Evan had wallowed in grief and buried himself in trans-forming the Circle A into the biggest and most suc-cessful ranch in the Torrence area.

"Then as long as you don't mind pitching in, I'll

drop Wade off with Anna and help Beth get dressed.''

Evan laid Maggie back on his lap. "Give the little tyke to me, son. You take Maggie to Anna." He reached up and wrapped his thumbs and index fingers around the baby's sturdy little chest and lifted him down, supporting Wade's still bobbling head with his fingertips. "Us guys will sit here in the rocker and discuss cattle futures," he told Jackson as his son scooped up the female half of his twins.

"Now, don't go corrupting my son with too much cattle talk," Jackson said with a chuckle in his voice. "The Circle A is well on its way to becoming half horse ranch."

Jackson looked ready for an argument despite the levity in his tone. Evan wondered how long it would take his son to believe he really did have final authority on the Circle A now. "*And* we'll talk about the quarter-horse market, too," Evan added, keeping his tone light. "Half and half. Right, little man? You go give Maggie to Anna and get that pretty wife of yours in to see Doc. We'll be fine."

Two hours later Jackson and Beth were back with an antibiotic prescription, two cases of formula and an abundant supply of bottles. "Doc wants the babies to be bottle-fed from here on," Jackson told him as he sat on the porch railing, again calming Wade.

"What does he say is wrong with Beth?"

"Doc thinks she picked up an infection during the

C-section and that the antibiotics should take care of it. But he doesn't want the twins nursing and getting the medication or tiring her. I think I'm going to call Mom to come and stay.''

Oh, terrific! Evan thought. Just what he needed. Flamboyant, busybody, know-it-all Meg Taggert descending and taking over his grandchildren. It was bad enough that she'd co-opted Jackson for nearly all of the past two years!

''Nonsense,'' he hastened to tell his son. ''We can handle two little babies with Anna's help. Beth won't want to miss her visit with Meg by not being up to par. Wait a while and see how it goes. In a month Beth will be up and around more and be ready to entertain.''

Jackson frowned. ''I wasn't only thinking of Beth. Anna has too much to do to take care of the babies and the house. And neither of you are here at night. Since this is slow season, I can do a lot to care for Beth, but still—I'd worry less if Mom came. Suppose we get hit with a blizzard like the one last spring? The men would need both you and me to get food to the cattle and that would leave Anna way overburdened. Besides all of that, once Mom hears about Beth being sick, I doubt wild horses could keep her away.''

''Then don't tell her. There's no sense in getting her all upset. She and Beth seem pretty close.''

''They are. And I know Beth wanted to be able to

entertain Mom while she's here.'' Jackson thought for a few seconds. ''Yeah, I guess you're right. I'll wait to tell her. If it looks as if we need her help, I'll call then. Otherwise she may change her current plan to go to Hawaii after her visit.''

Well, it wasn't much, but it was at least a temporary reprieve. The Wicked Witch of the East wouldn't be landing for a while anyway!

Meg took a sip of her hot tea as she took a break from sorting through the options the travel brochures portrayed in dazzling color. She glanced out of the sunroom through the floor-to-ceiling windows. Her gaze swept past the stone terrace to Laurel Glen's fenced pastures and snow-covered fields. Then on to the distant tree line, bare now except for the evergreens.

This was her favorite place in Laurel House. It had been her sanctuary for years. She'd decorated it with white wicker furniture, rattan tables and lattice accents. The cushions on the settee and chairs were a cheery yellow and white, along with the pots that held a profusion of plants.

She sighed. It was her sanctuary no longer, because she'd moved to what had traditionally been the cottage Laurel Glen's trainer occupied so her brother, his wife and their growing family could have Laurel House to themselves.

She'd stayed in the house last night only because

Laurel House had been the site of the big Valentine's dance Ross sponsored every year. This year, with Amelia expecting her second child any day, Ross had been concerned that the morning-after arrangements to dismantle the party preparations would be too much on his very pregnant wife. Meg had volunteered to see to the workmen and keep it all running smoothly. And she had. She'd been doing it for years. In fact, she'd acted as Ross's hostess from the first party until he'd married Amelia.

Meg's life was changing as much as Ross's had since meeting Amelia, but in vastly different ways. Jack, Meg's long-lost son, had found her and she was now making plans to visit him, his wife and infant twins. She was a grandmother even though she didn't feel a day over twenty. She smiled, remembering her grandmother saying that her body might be eighty but her mind was still nineteen. Meg finally understood. But, of course, she was only fifty-two and she wouldn't go back to her anguishing nineteenth year for anything. That was the year she had still been grieving for Wade and the baby whom circumstances had forced her to give up for adoption.

Banishing sad thoughts, Meg picked up a Hawaiian cruise brochure, the strongest possibility. Since she was already going to be in Colorado, it only seemed prudent to use her visit with Jack, Beth and the twins as a jumping-off point for some interesting place that would ordinarily be too far for her usual midwinter trip. Meg often went on a cruise to the Caribbean, but cruises had begun to get old. Or so she'd thought. A cruise from California to Hawaii with stop-offs at several of the smaller islands in the Hawaiian chain, however, put a new light on it.

Ross and Amelia's precocious eighteen-month-old, Laurel, charged into the sunroom, her mouth going as fast as her feet. Meg managed to pick out only one of the babbled words. "Slow down, little one. What are you telling Aunty Meg?"

"Unca Jack. Gib him ta you."

"Give him to me?" Meg noticed the cordless phone then. Laurel had it by the antenna. She'd probably dragged it along the ground on her way there. She chuckled. "Thank you, sweetie," she said as Laurel climbed up on the settee with her and tucked herself against Meg's side. "I imagine Uncle Jack's hearing will be impaired for the rest of the day." Meg took the phone, and just then Amelia stuck her head in.

"Sorry, Meg. She got away from me."

Amelia looked done in. "No problem. Come put your feet up, and after I talk to Jack we'll have a chat." She put the phone to her ear. "Jack, darling. How good to hear from you. Can you hear me at all or has Laurel deafened you?"

"Mom—" His voice wobbled and her heart just about stopped. Then she heard him take a deep breath before he began again. "We have a problem here,

Mom,'' he said finally, worry rife in his voice. "Beth's in the hospital."

"Oh, Lord have mercy. What happened?"

"She got a fever about a week after she came home. Doc Reynolds put her on an antibiotic, but she kept spiking high fevers at night. He tried a stronger one, and it seemed to work for a few days, then her fever spiked again last night."

"Who is taking care of the twins? Anna?"

"Actually, Dad's taking care of them. Anna has the flu."

That *man* was caring for her precious grandchildren! By himself? Oh, this just wouldn't do. It wouldn't do at all! "Why on earth didn't you call me before now? I'd have been there in a flash."

"Well, that's why I'm calling now. I've been taking care of Beth and the twins at night by myself, but with her in the hospital..." He huffed out a tired sigh. "I can't keep burning the candle at both ends, and I need to be at the hospital with her. She's so weak, Mom. I'm hoping your cruise plans aren't written in stone yet. Do you think you could stay indefinitely?"

Mentally consigning Hawaii to the trash can, she said, "Nothing in my life is written in stone, especially where people I love are concerned. I'll leave on the first flight I can get out of here and rent something at the airport after I land. Don't dare consider picking me up at the airport. You have enough on your plate right now.'' And don't even think of sending Evan to fetch me, either, she longed to add, but didn't.

''You're sure?''

''Well, of course I'm sure. What on earth do you think a mother is for? I wish I understood why you didn't call me sooner,'' she said again. ''Goodness, son, you know how important you all are to me.''

''Dad thought it'd be better to wait till Beth was on her feet the way she wanted to be when you got here. But now I'm not even sure she's going to get better.''

''She's going to be fine. Don't start doubting that.''

It nearly broke Meg's heart to hear tears in her son's voice. ''They don't know what's wrong, Mom. And she just keeps getting weaker.'' He paused, she thought to compose himself. ''I'm so afraid of losing her.''

Meg sought to reassure him and remind him to lean on the Lord. ''Just hang on to your faith, darling. The Lord has a plan. Even in this. What hospital is she in, and what room number? You know how everyone here is going to worry and want to at least send flowers. Have you called her brother?''

While Jack answered her questions, Meg made plans. For the first time in months she felt energized. Someone needed her again.

Chapter Two

Meg's first stop after landing in Denver was the hospital in Greeley. She didn't really know what she expected to find when she peeked in Beth's door, but it wasn't her daughter-in-law looking as if she were knocking on death's door. Thin and wan, Beth lay sleeping in her bed. The muted sunlight filtering through the drawn shade at the window made her light blond hair glint with an unearthly glow. For one second Meg felt fear overcome her. Was she too late?

Then she saw Beth's chest move, but it was clear her breathing was shallow. The thought of Jack, and all of them, losing her was too immense.

Dear Lord, I don't know what You're up to, but please don't let Beth die. I don't want Jack to feel that kind of pain. I know he's up to the test, but he's been alone for so many years.

"Mom?" Jack said from the hall behind her.

Meg whirled and held out her arms. Jack hugged her for all he was worth. "How is she doing?" she asked.

Jack stepped back and shook his head, tears in his eyes. He took her hand and pulled her from the room, closing the door behind them. Across the hall was a sun-drenched solarium. He led her in there, and they both sat on the wide slate windowsills overlooking the snow that covered the area. It was clear Jack needed to unload.

"She's not getting better, Mom," he said, sounding stuffed up from fighting tears. His eyes were red rimmed from the moments when he'd obviously failed. "This morning there was a doctor from the CDC in with her when I got here. He said it looks like something he called a superbug. That means it's resisting conventional antibiotics. He had them change her medication again. I don't think I've ever been more afraid in my life."

"How are Beth's spirits holding up?"

Jack winced and looked away out the window. "Before she fell asleep about an hour ago, she made me promise to find a mother for the twins."

"I hope you told her what utter nonsense that is."

"I did but she just kept insisting."

Meg sighed. "So you promised."

Jack shook his head, pursing his lips, and still stubbornly fought the tears pooling in his eyes. "I told her I'd never find anyone else, so she'd better start planning to make a full recovery."

Ah, that was her stubborn son talking. "Well, good for you!"

"It feels like a nightmare," he whispered, and turned to lean the back of his head against the cool glass pane. "Three weeks ago we were the two happiest people in the world. And now I'm losing her."

Meg straightened and stood in front of him. "Jack, look at me." He opened his eyes. "You are *not* losing her," she insisted. "And just to make sure, I called Pastor Jim and he's started a prayer chain. All your friends at the Tabernacle are praying for Beth. Until we call and say she's better, not a minute will go by that someone won't be praying for her. Tabernacle members are strong prayer warriors, son. They won't let you down, and neither will God. Now you go back to your wife, and when she wakes up again, it's your job to convince her that this is a fight worth winning. I'm going on to the ranch so you two can concentrate on getting Beth well. You tell her I was here, and that I said she's to stop this gloomy talk about leaving you behind. And tell her I'll come see her soon to make sure her attitude has changed."

Jack grinned a little and stood to hug her again. "That alone should scare her into getting better. I love you, Mom. I thank God every day for letting me find you."

She stepped back and cupped his cheek. "And I

thank Him for leading you back to me, son. Now, you take care of our Beth, and I'll see to those grand-babies of mine.''

"Mom," Jack said as he raked his fingers nervously through his hair. "Uh…could you take it easy on Dad? He really has tried these last months. He did everything he promised to do about the Circle A. And he's been a rock through this since Beth got sick.''

Meg blinked. She'd have to brush up on her acting skills. Jack wasn't supposed to have noticed her hostility toward Evan Alton. She smiled sweetly. "Why, darling, if you have no problem with Evan, why should I? I'm here to relieve him. That's all.''

Jack nodded, but he didn't seem completely convinced. She'd have to work harder at masking her dislike for the man her son called father. As far as Meg was concerned, Evan Alton had been a poor substitute for Wade Jackson. Wade would have thrown himself into fatherhood the way he'd done with everything else in his life. She had to fight a little twinge of anger at him. Perhaps if he hadn't seen himself as invincible he wouldn't have re-enlisted, and he'd have lived to be the father her son had deserved.

Soon she was following the directions Jack had given her to the ranch. As promised, it took her through the center of Torrence, then meandered across the countryside to the entrance of the Circle A. Hanging on a wooden crossbeam across the narrow road was a carved sign reading "Circle A Ranch."

"Welcome to the Wild West, pardner," Meg drawled, and turned onto the private gravel road. "I guess this is the Circle A."

After a mile she came to the first building. It was the ranch-style house she'd seen in Jack's pictures. It appeared to be a long one-story log home but a deeply pitched roof added a second floor at the rear. Different as it was from Laurel House, Meg was charmed by its rustic simplicity. From Jack's description and the odd snapshot from Christmas, she pictured the interior with its rustic beamed cathedral ceiling and a balcony edged with artfully twisted branches that had been used to fashion a sturdy railing.

The squared-off logs used in the construction of the walls and the rustic red clay tile roof above them did nothing to alter her perception of rustic comfort. Now that she saw the building "in person," it reminded her of the side view of a faceted jewel—a ruby.

Big terra-cotta pots planted with specimen trees, which Jack had mentioned in letters, dotted a patio edged with a red-stone wall. A patio and wall surrounded the house and she saw that the wall was topped with a thick layer of snow. Towering elms lined the outside of the wall and patio, giving the house a nestled-in feel. The bare branches of all the trees were ice coated and glistened in the strong winter sunlight, adding to the jewel-like quality of the home.

In the distance she could see more squat buildings and several corrals. The other buildings all matched the house as far as construction and color went, but the roofs with their shallower pitches were slightly snow covered. The heart of the Circle A operation seemed to have settled in for a long winter, just as Laurel Glen had back home.

As she tooled along next to the house, she noticed several work vehicles parked in a circular parking area just beyond the house that Jack had mentioned. Meg pulled in there, turned off the engine and got out. Her boots crunched in the dry snow as she walked toward a stone path that led to the back door.

The air was crisp and dry, so unlike most winter days in the east, where higher humidity levels made summer seem hotter and winter feel colder. The icicles dripping from the eaves of the house shone like diamonds in the sun. Her analogy of seeing the house as a ruby made more sense than ever. It really did glisten.

Meg stopped halfway up the path, her heart pounding. She would have to face *him* in a moment. She didn't understand it, but something about the tall, handsome man with the iron-gray hair and commanding presence—her adversary, Evan Alton—undid her. She couldn't face him like this. Then it occurred to her that there was something she hadn't done since leaving the hospital. More important, there was Someone she needed to lean on.

"Lord," she prayed aloud. "I praise You for being my Father. And I beg forgiveness for not leaning on You. I ask You to give me strength and patience with this man who has so disappointed me, for my child's sake. And, again, please bless Jack, Beth and the twins with the return of her good health. If there is a lesson here for one or all of us, let it be learned from her illness and not her death."

Feeling better able to face Evan Alton on his home turf, Meg walked the rest of the way up the path and across the stone patio. As with most homes in rural areas, the door was unlocked, so she opened it. She stepped into a homey kitchen with soapstone counters and back splashes and natural-colored, pine bead-board cabinet fronts.

Any other impressions she got were short-circuited somewhere on their way to her brain by the troubling cries of what sounded like a dozen babies. They sounded hungry. Good grief! Had the man abandoned the twins?

Meg quickly followed the wails to a sprawling sitting room with the vaulted ceiling she'd expected. And there she discovered a sight more startling than walking in on all that howling.

Evan Alton sat in a rocker with a baby on each shoulder, attempting to burp both fussy babies at the same time. "Come on, you two," he was saying in a low voice that even she had to admit had a soothing quality to it. "You've got to stop conspiring against your granddad. One little burp. I promise. Just co-operate and we'll get you back to the feedbag."

"Well, this is a photo op the local newspaper editor would probably kill for," Meg drawled. "The great and powerful Evan Alton brought low by four-teen pounds of newborn."

"Do you always walk right into a man's home and attack him with your smart-mouthed comments?" he demanded.

"If and when I attack, you'll know it. As for the house, I was invited. And I was under the impression that this was Jack and Beth's home now. Or did you renege on that promise, too?"

"I have never once reneged on a promise to my son."

Meg waited a beat, raised one dark eyebrow and said, "No, just on several to his mother."

He shook his head. "Nope. Not to Martha, either."

She clenched her teeth. "I was referring to *me*."

The twins, who had stopped their crying when she'd spoken, apparently got bored with the sound of a new voice and started bawling again. "I assume you've come to help," Evan said over the din. "So help. Take Maggie. She's the easier to handle."

"Are you implying that I can't handle Wade?"

"No, I'm saying it right out plain and simple. He's

having a problem with the bottle, poor little tyke. I'm not turning him over to some inexperienced second stringer who's never done more with a baby than give him away.''

Oh! Meg folded her arms over her chest. ''I wish I'd known then that you have no real respect for adoption. But you lied through your teeth to hide your feelings.''

''I didn't lie,'' Evan said emphatically. ''I hold adoption and the ability to love someone else's offspring as one of the finer qualities humans have. It's the parent discarding a child I still have trouble with. Especially when they turn around and storm back into the lives of those children three decades later, disrupting everything.''

Meg snatched up the infant in pink from his shoulder, and the bottle with the pink charm from the table next to him. ''If you'll remember, Jack came looking for me. It seems there was a void in his life he hoped I could fill. It isn't my fault he felt that way. It's yours.''

Evan gritted his teeth as Meg Taggert settled in the other rocker at the far side of the hearth. He'd probably ground a year's worth of enamel off his teeth when she'd arched her dark eyebrow in that superior way of hers. Blast the platinum-haired witch! Knowing she was right really stuck in his craw.

Evan smirked in spite of his annoyance. For some reason, matching wits with her always made him feel more alive than he had in the years before meeting her. "It must really get your goat that Jack chose to come back and run the Circle A and live here with me over Laurel Glen and that foreman's job your brother gave him."

Again that annoying but lovely eyebrow arched. "Ross didn't *give* Jack a thing. He earned that position on his own merit. My brother hired Jack with no knowledge whatever of who he was. In fact, I was away at the time. Doesn't it bother you that Ross saw the potential in Jack during a one-hour interview when you never had, even after living a lifetime with him?"

Evan arched his eyebrow in a mocking parody of her own expression. "I knew his potential," he drawled. "He and I differed on the future of the ranch. It was Jackson who cut and ran. I finally decided that if I'd worked for years to build this ranch to where it was for his and Cris's future, it was time he take over the reins and relieve me of the burden. That's the difference between you and me. I've admitted my mistakes. You just keep living a lie, usurping other people's children and flitting around the world when real life bores you or gets too tough."

"Odd that you feel qualified to assess my life when yours has been such a dismal parody of really living. At least I've been there for the people who needed me and I haven't spent over a year in therapy only to continue lying to myself. You weren't building this ranch for the kids. You worked yourself 24/7 so you wouldn't have time to feel anything and so you'd be the great big fish in this little tiny pond called Torrence." She stood, shaking the empty baby bottle. "Now that Maggie has finished this, I'll change her and put her in her bed. Don't bother showing me the way. I'll just poke around till I come to the nursery."

With that she floated from the room, leaving him with hundreds of comebacks erupting in his brain when it was too late to use any of them. And she left him with a terrible, hollow feeling about his obsession with the ranch and about his life for the past twenty-five or so years. He couldn't deny that he hadn't actually *felt* anything for years. Nothing but the loss of Martha and the fear of losing the children she'd prized above all else. Was that why he'd held them at an emotional distance all those years?

He hadn't thought himself such a coward.

Chapter Three

Watching from the window at the end of the second-floor balcony, Evan saw Meg Taggert heft her big suitcase out of the trunk of her rental car, extend the handle and drag it behind her awkwardly up the uneven path toward the house. He tried not to feel small and mean, but it wasn't working.

If she'd asked for his help, he'd have given it to her without a thought, but they hadn't spoken a word to each other since he'd gone into the nursery to change Wade's diaper, only to find that she'd rearranged the shelf above the dressing table. He always kept the baby wipes in the same place, between the rash ointment and the powder. That way they were at his fingertips in those moments when seconds counted.

She'd carelessly tossed off his complaint, saying

she hadn't rearranged a thing. She just hadn't remembered where everything went. So he'd patiently explained about having a place for everything and everything in its place so that changing two diapers before feeding the twins went more quickly. Twins changed certain moments of child care from a one-person labor of love to an assembly-line mentality. Bottles were made in twos. Bottoms were diapered in twos. Baths were a dual affair, as well. And these two, though male and female, were exactly the same in every way except for Wade's bottle problems. So if there was no organization there was instant chaos, because they both wanted everything at the same time. And like their grandmother they weren't long on patience!

The thump-thump of that heavy suitcase on the stairs shook him out of his reverie. He watched for a long moment as she struggled with the weight on the steps, then couldn't let it go any longer. Evan turned from the window. "Here, let me get that," he groused, then went down the wide stairs to stand next to her.

"I'm fine," she said, and kept pulling it up by the handle, the wheels giving her no help on the steps.

He held out his hand to take the handle, but she showed no signs of relinquishing her burden. "Don't be a fool," he told her. "You aren't going to do the twins any good in traction."

"I'm a lot stronger than I look. And don't let the hair fool you. I can run rings around you."

Maybe her hair was more prematurely white than platinum, but there was still a golden glow of youth to the color and shaggy cut that brushed her long, graceful neck. Maybe that was what had kept him thinking of it as glamorous rather than an effect of aging. Or maybe it was her pretty and still unlined face. He looked at her, taking in her lithe figure and the unmatched determination in her bluer-than-blue eyes.

For years he'd been coming up against that same stubborn pride reflected in his son's nearly identical eyes. He sighed, not doubting her stamina or her determination to have things her way. "No, woman, you just look like someone who's bitten off more than she can chew with that steamer trunk. And you look like someone who's going to put her back out. Now, let me carry that before we wake the twins arguing about something so stupid."

She nodded and let him grab the second handle on the side. "It's a suitcase. Not a steamer trunk." She must have felt the need to explain. "I have gifts for the twins and I may be on my way to Hawaii after Beth is on the mend. I had to pack for two climates."

He snapped the handle back in at the top and hefted the oversize case up the steps. He couldn't believe she'd gotten it as far as she had. "How long did you plan for Beth to be sick? A year?"

"If you ever left your little kingdom," she drawled, "you'd know there's a large variety of activities on a cruise ship that all require different types of clothing. Plus we always dress for dinner at Laurel House. So I needed winter clothes for meals here, too."

"Well, la-de-da. This isn't Laurel Glen. Here, we eat in the breakfast room, or in the bunk house with the men, and sometimes even out on the range. Don't go trying to impose your snooty ideas on us."

She went on as if he hadn't spoken. "As well as clothes for hospital visits and everyday wear while caring for the twins and the house." Then she added one of her signature little zingers, proving she'd heard him after all. "Oh, don't worry. I'm not here to civilize you. I never take on an impossible task. I just intend to take care of the twins until Beth is able."

"I don't remember asking for help with them."

"I know. In fact, you talked Jack out of calling me when he should have. If he had, he wouldn't be an emotional and physical wreck right now from trying to cope all alone every night. By the way, I also noticed just how well you were doing on your own when I arrived."

Was the woman ever wrong? He decided to just ignore the comment. A wise choice, since this time he couldn't think of a single comeback.

"Your room will be here," he said instead of admitting to that embarrassing truth. He carted the suitcase in and dropped it on the double bed. "There's a private bath through that door."

"What's wrong with the one next to the nursery?"

"I'm staying in there so I can hear the babies in the night."

"I thought I'd take care of the twins' middle-of-the-night feeding."

"If you really came to help, you can take Maggie, and I'll take Wade. That way Jackson might sleep through the night if he comes home at all. I would have been over here before Beth was hospitalized if he'd let me. But telling Jackson what to do hasn't worked since he was two years old. Or haven't you noticed how stubborn he is?"

There was the most annoying light of pride in her eyes when she tipped her chin and said, "Oh, I've noticed. It's a Taggert family trait. Now, if you'll excuse me, I'd like to change out of these travel clothes before the twins wake again. Have you thought about dinner yet?"

"There's a casserole defrosting," he said, and turned away. "This isn't Laurel Glen. I hope Your Majesty can adapt to something simpler than five-course meals served in a dining room," he muttered.

Meg balled her hands into fists and flopped onto the bed as the door snicked closed behind maddening, infuriating, annoying Evan Alton. She uncurled her hands and let them rest on her flat stomach. She was strung so tight she felt as if she were about to explode. What had happened to all her noble intentions?

She'd taken one look at him looking exasperated but unruffled by those hysterical, frightening infants and she'd gotten all defensive on him—after all, the best defense is a good offense. So she'd gone on the attack. There was nothing else to call what she had done. She closed her eyes and fervently prayed, *Lord, help me get rid of this awful anger.*

The distressed cries of the babies woke Meg from a sound sleep. Looking at the clock on the bedside table, its digital numbers glowing green in the darkness, she realized she'd slept for over an hour. Then another spate of cries sent her into action. In record time she changed into carefully ironed jeans and a sky-blue-and-white ski sweater, then slipped into a pair of docksiders before going off to beard the Colorado lion in his den. Or the nursery, in this case.

"Now, what's all this caterwauling?" she said in a sunny tone as she breezed into the adorable nursery.

Beth and Jack had done the room half pink and half blue above, and below a border with a white background. The well-known nursery-rhyme characters in the border cavorted along on a soft blanket of crisp green grass.

"I told her you two are like this," Evan said as he fastened the tab on Wade's diaper. "You both want changing at the same time. And feeding and bouncing. A full-time job is what you two are,'' he said, speaking more to the baby than her. ''Now that Meg is here, she can change sister Maggie and Granddad can feed you right away. Doesn't that work out just swell?'' He lifted Wade off the changing table and into his arms, then walked toward the doorway.

''If you're going to speak using the children as a filter, kindly refer to me as Grandmom. I don't want them confused,'' she said to his back. He stopped, his shoulders stiffening, then he walked forward. ''Do you hear that, Wade? She wants to be called Grandmom. Who'd have thought a woman who'd never been called Mom until a couple of years ago would be ready for grandchildren? We'll have to remember that, won't we?''

Meg gritted her teeth. ''Did you see him, Maggie?'' she asked the fussy infant as she lifted her from the pretty white cradle that was all decked out in a soft pink. Wade's white cradle was dressed identically, but in blue. ''Did you see that superior expression he was wearing? Remember this, dear one. Handsome men are the ones we all want at first glance, but my, are they an arrogant lot. They start out sweet and smiling. But once we get to know them, we figure it out. They can't hide their true selves for very long. The trick is to get to know them and not love them. That one, well, he won't be a problem for me, but just you watch yourself, or he'll be running your life.'' Maggie cooed and Meg laughed. ''Me. Oh, don't worry about me where he's concerned. So far I haven't been able to handle being in the room with that one for two minutes, so how could I find time to fall for him?'' She glanced toward the door Evan had exited minutes earlier. ''But he is handsome. I'll give him that. And your daddy was wrong. He says his daddy's eyes are blue, but they aren't. They're as gray as a snow-laden sky. Nope, not blue at all.''

Meg heard someone talking in the nursery at the ungodly hour of four-thirty the next morning. The twins had been up between one and two, and she and Evan had once again divided the care duties and kept them from waking Jack, who'd come in around midnight looking tired and more than a little defeated. Beth showed no signs of improvement from the change in medication.

As Meg tossed on her robe, she counted out the usual three-and-a-half-hour span between feedings. If the twins had awakened, they were up early and had been unusually quiet in their demands for once.

But when she opened her door, she let out a sigh. It was Jack talking in a low timbre to one or both of his children. As quietly as she could, Meg crept to the door that was slightly ajar and peered inside. Jack sat in a glider that had clearly been bought for Beth's frame and not her son's wide-shouldered build. He held both twins, one in each arm, as they slept the sleep of the innocent in their father's embrace.

"She really misses you two," he was saying. "I'm going to download those pictures I just took and blow them up to poster size. That way every time Mommy opens her pretty green eyes she'll see the best reason I know for her to fight to get better. Daddy's going to miss you two, but I've decided to stay near the hospital to be with Mommy. I know it's important for me to be with you two, but right now Mommy needs me there to be strong for her. Grandmom and Granddad are here for you, so I know you'll be fine. But you both have to be good for them."

Meg couldn't handle the heartbreaking scene for another moment. She started to turn away, but the floor gave a telltale squeak, giving away her presence. Jack looked up and their eyes met.

"Mom. Join us. The kids and I were just having a chat. I guess you heard. I'm going to take a room at the motel near the hospital so I can be with Beth more."

"That's a good idea, Jack," she said, and walked to stand next to him. With a hand on his shoulder she continued, "Beth really does need you right now. Your father and I will be fine here with Maggie and Wade." Meg tilted her head, looking down on the sweet faces of the infants in Jack's arms. "My, but Maggie looks like Beth."

Jack smiled. "Except her coloring is all Taggert.

Who does Wade look like, do you think? He has Beth's blond hair, but…''

Meg shook her head, feeling a poignant tug on her heartstrings. It seemed that history—or more truthfully, the Lord—had a way of righting inequities. ''He has Wade's hair. Actually he looks exactly like his grandfather. Right down to that little dimple in his chin. I'd keep him away from helicopters, if I were you. And most definitely the hayloft. Your father apparently tried to fly sans chopper when he was seven.'' She chuckled, remembering Wade's boyish smile as he told her about that chapter of his too-short life. ''He broke both his legs and several ribs. He swore he'd still have been grounded if his parents hadn't been killed when he was in his teens.''

''You loved him a lot.'' Jack paused. ''But isn't it time, Mom?''

Meg frowned. ''Time?''

''Time to start living life for yourself and not everyone else.''

Chapter Four

Evan heard the babies whimper, and tossed back his covers as he glanced at the clock. Eight o'clock! The babies had done well, sleeping since two. He nearly stepped into the hall half-dressed, but at the last moment he remembered the presence of Meg Taggert in the house. Martha's house. He shook his head as he stepped into his jeans. It was Jackson's house. Jackson and Beth's house now.

His daughter, Crystal, had moved to Pennsylvania to marry a state police detective. She'd embraced the East every bit as much as his daughter-in-law had embraced Colorado's high plains. Over Jackson's objections, Cris had insisted Jackson take ownership of the ranch and house, agreeing to take a higher percentage of the profits each year as payment.

It hadn't really surprised Evan. His daughter had

been restless for some time before her trip east. And her love for the big blond Pennsylvania State Police detective was obvious. Still, though he was happy for her, he missed Crystal and regretted not being able to get to know his grandchildren when they came along.

"Good morning, darlings," he heard the Taggert woman saying to the twins as he stepped into the hall. For some reason her alto voice soothed them once again, and the usual morning caterwauling stopped immediately. "Let's see which of you I should take care of first. Eenie meanie minie moe..."

Evan grinned when both twins started squalling. So much for her magical effect. He guessed he'd be magnanimous and ride to the rescue. After all, once Beth was on the mend, Meg Taggert would hop her broom and ride off into the sunset. And Evan would be right there on the Circle A with his grandchildren—hers, too.

"What are you two going on about?" he said, breezing into the nursery. "Did your grandmother pinch you? Or are you just figuring out she's in on the conspiracy to keep you from getting to the food?"

"Evan! Good morning," she said in an all-too-sunny voice. He might have known she'd be one of those morning people. "I thought I'd take care of Wade this time. I'm not going to get to know my grandson if you're always the one doing things for him.''

Evan thought about not warning her about the effect the cool air had on little Wade, but his conscience got the better of him. He hated mornings too much to ruin someone else's day. "Fine," he agreed, "but have the diaper ready or you'll get your morning shower early."

Meg actually blushed. "Oh. Well. Uh…thank you for mentioning that."

For the first time Evan understood the late Wade Jackson's attraction to Meg Taggert. But only if you overlooked her grating personality, her superior attitude and her high-society ways. She was quite pretty with her cheeks all aglow. Really, he had to admit she was a beautiful woman. Her hair, while white, didn't make her look old at all but exotically attractive. Maybe it was its youthfully shaggy cut or just the personality it reflected. And that vibrant, exotic quality was only enhanced by her sapphire eyes. All in all it was a startling combination.

More startling, though, was the simple fact that he'd even noticed. He frowned as he realized Meg had said something while his thoughts had drifted into an uncomfortable zone. "'Scuse me, ma'am?" he said.

Meg, he noticed, worked quickly and efficiently, removing Wade's diaper and wiping the baby down.

"I asked if you usually bathe the children before breakfast. They didn't get a bath at bedtime."

"Beth likes to do it before their morning nap. It relaxes them."

She shrugged and went to work rapidly taping on a new diaper. "I'd have thought a bath would wake them up."

"Me, too, but they're Beth's babies, so I do things as close to how she did them as possible. I'm holding on to the belief that she'll be back here to raise them."

Those blue, blue eyes of Meg's filled with tears and she bit her full bottom lip. "Oh, I pray you're right, Evan. In these last several years Beth has become the daughter I never had. Poor Jack looked so discouraged and frightened when I saw him earlier this morning. He's terrified to leave her side at all. That's why he decided to take a motel room and stay in Greeley. So he can be near her and give her all his energy."

Evan frowned. "What are you talking about?"

She nodded. "I heard him in here talking to the babies in the middle of the night. He'd been taking their picture to hang in Beth's room. It's so hard to watch him go through this when all I can do is stand on the sidelines and pray."

"He's not coming home? And he didn't see fit to tell me?"

"Really, Evan. I just told you how nervous he is

about leaving Beth. He must have gone back to the hospital while we were still asleep. I'm sure he meant no slight to you.''

Hurt that Jackson had spoken to her about his decision and not him, Evan retaliated. ''What about the Circle A? I turned the ranch over to him and now he just dumps it back in my lap without so much as a word?''

As soon as Meg's eyes lit like twin blue flames, Evan realized that in his pain he'd said the wrong thing. When would he ever break that awful habit?

''He didn't dump anything on you,'' she retorted sharply. ''He said Seth knows how to get in touch with him if there's a problem. He thought we would take care of the twins together, with Seth handling the ranch. Through some miracle you managed to raise Jack with some good solid values. You should be thankful. At least Jack chose to 'abandon' a piece of real estate for a loved one in need. You abandoned two helpless children who needed you in favor of building an empire. A mighty sorry trade-off, if you ask me, Evan.'' She picked up Wade, all diapered and fresh smelling, and floated from the room.

''Who asked you?'' Evan growled under his breath, drawing a cute little-baby scowl from Maggie. ''Oh, not you, too, angel. Has the Wicked Witch of the East got you under her spell already?''

Maggie made an adorable little cooing sound, startling him. Saddening him. A first, and both Jackson and Beth had missed it. His greatest fear was that Beth was destined to miss them all. Not wanting to project his gloomy mood onto Maggie, he started a one-way conversation with his granddaughter. "Well, fine. I'll give you that she's pretty, but pretty is as pretty does." He sighed and undid the tapes on Maggie's diaper. "For crying out loud. What does that mean, anyway?" he asked the now silent angel on the dressing table staring up at him with her navy blue eyes wide and interested. "Look how old your granddad is starting to sound. I'm using expressions that always drove me crazy." He glanced out the hall door, then looked back at the baby to say in a sing-song voice that didn't reflect his current rancor, "But then again, maybe that woman's already driven me around the bend. I guess I should consider that, huh, baby girl?"

When he joined Meg in the kitchen, he found she had heated Maggie's bottle along with Wade's. It was nice to see she hadn't taken her pique out on the children, but then to be honest he couldn't imagine her doing such a thing. She seemed to have goodwill toward everyone—but him.

"Till Anna's up and about, we'll have to fend for ourselves," he said as he tested the bottle. "I'm not much of a cook. How about you? Oh, forget I asked. Laurel Glen has a cook, right?"

Meg looked up at him, and again he was struck by her beauty. He wondered why she'd never married.

Why she didn't color her hair. If she did, Meg Taggert wouldn't look a day over forty. There were no lines around her eyes or her mouth. Her figure was downright girlish. Her hair was absolutely the only feature she had that put her in the middle-aged category.

"I haven't always eaten at Laurel House. In fact, I live in the trainer's cottage and fend for myself most nights now."

"How come you don't color your hair?" he blurted out, and then wasn't sure who was more shocked by the question.

Thoroughly surprised by the question, Meg blinked. No one had ever asked why she left her hair white. They just accepted her as she was. "Why? Are you saying I look old?"

"Do you always take offense this easily?" Evan demanded. "I asked because if you colored it, you'd look more than ten years younger than you are. I thought that's what most women wanted."

Now, that was annoying! He was right. Looking younger was probably something most women wanted. So why didn't she care? She stared at him, searching for an answer. It wasn't as if she dressed like some outmoded matron. Her clothes were classic and timeless. And she was certainly as active as, if not more than, most forty-year-olds.

"Was that a compliment?" she asked, pushing aside troubling questions. "I'm sorry. I must admit

I've never thought about it. Maybe I will, though I'm just not sure I care all that much.''

Evan shrugged. ''No need to think too much on it. It just struck me, so I mentioned it. Guess that's what happens when you live with men.''

Now, wasn't that typical of Evan Alton! ''Crystal wasn't a man. Not in the least.''

Evan grimaced. ''You just love pointing out all my mistakes, don't you? For the record, I know I made mistakes. I've told my children I'm sorry and have tried to make up for it. They've forgiven me. And I don't care if you do, because the past is between me and my kids.''

Oh, he had an answer for everything, didn't he? Well, let him try to wiggle out of this one! ''But the promises you made to me didn't count? Is that it? I gave you my child to raise.''

''*Gave* being the operative word. You tried to take him back, but it didn't work. Instead Beth lives here now, too, which must get your goat.''

His look said he hoped it did. She was about to retaliate when little Wade let out a wail. He didn't seem to be in pain. Just upset. She had to think he'd picked up on her mood. Meg stood. ''I'm taking him to the nursery. Then I'll give him his bath.'' She looked at the clock. ''I'll meet you here at ten. And we'll settle this out of the twins' presence. This can't go on, Evan, or these children will be absolutely ruined before Beth comes home. Don't try to put it off by hiding from me, either. Because, mister, I have some things to say to you and I'll hunt you down to say them. And I'm sure you have things to say to me, considering all the little darts you keep throwing. Maybe if we just get it all out in the open, we can work together to care for these children as they deserve. They don't need an atmosphere of anger and hostility any more than my son deserved the childhood you gave him.''

She left it at that, and only realized when she left the room that she was crying and had been since he'd implied that she'd abandoned Jack. When she found it difficult to see the stairs as she climbed to the second level she sat on a step and just held Wade as she'd never had the chance to hold his father.

She didn't need this on top of worry over Beth. She really didn't.

Chapter Five

Meg returned to the kitchen precisely at ten o'clock. Evan was standing at the back door gazing out. "Jackson called," he said, still looking out. "Beth's no better on the new medication. He said he couldn't sleep for worry, so he left to head on back to Greeley and the hospital. Did he tell you she tried to get him to promise to marry again?"

Meg sat against the big, scarred trestle table and crossed her arms. "I hope you didn't unload on him about not seeing you first before he left."

He whirled. "What kind of person do you take me for?"

"The unfeeling kind. The kind who can't understand that an eighteen-year-old girl could love her child so much that she'd give him up for his own good!"

Evan crossed his arms, his expression more belligerent than before. "Oh, and a career on Broadway had nothing to do with it?"

She felt like stamping her foot, but refused to give up her dignity for this...this cowboy. "No, Evan. Wanting to get back to my career was *not* why I put him up for adoption. Ask yourself if I'd have given up my own child for a career, only to leave it years later. By then I was completely established, but I left it to help my brother raise his children. Have you even talked to Jack about this?"

"I...no." Evan leaned against the open doorway. "Jackson hasn't shared a bit of it with me. And I guess that's partly my fault. In the beginning, when he first found you, I didn't want to discuss it. I know Wade Jackson was a helicopter pilot in Vietnam. He died leaving you pregnant. And I suppose I know you were engaged to him, since you left that ring for Jackson. I figured if you could hand over both the baby and the ring, you didn't care much about either of them."

"Well, you couldn't have been more wrong!" She stood and paced to the opposite end of the big country kitchen. She needed to get away from him. Something about him put her on edge even when he wasn't being aggravating.

Staring into the fire in the oversize stone fireplace, she explained in a measured tone, not wanting her reaction to him to color the conversation. "I had nowhere to turn. My father had disowned me because I wanted to dance."

"Can't say as I blame him. I wouldn't want my daughter parading half-naked on stage."

Meg turned around and shook her head. She'd tried. She really had. "You would have gotten along wonderfully with my father. Both pigheaded cowboys jumping to judgment over something you know nothing about. I was never half-naked! You kept the *Hello, Dolly!* playbill I left for Jack. I was dressed for the gay nineties! Did you never get out of this podunk little town long enough to see it or any play from that era. I wasn't in *Hair!* I was in *Fiddler on the Roof.* We wore turn-of-the-century Russian peasant costumes! And my last show on Broadway before I went on the road with a touring company was *Shenandoah.* I was covered neck to ankle in antebellum gowns."

Evan pursed his lips and stood straighter. "You still gave him away instead of keeping him."

Meg took a deep breath, searching for calm. It slipped out of reach. "It isn't called giving *away.* It's called giving *up* for adoption for a reason. I gave Jack up even though I wanted to keep him because I wanted him to have the kind of life Wade and I would have given him. Wade was raised on a ranch, and even though he'd been orphaned, the ranch was waiting for him after Vietnam, but I had no claim on it. I grew up on a horse farm surrounded by family, but I couldn't go home.''

''So you're saying you did it for him?''

He sounded so skeptical. She threw up her hands. ''What kind of life would Jack have had with a single mother? I didn't want my baby raised with no family and a mother too exhausted to give him her all. I didn't want him to suffer the stigma of illegitimacy. I'd accepted the Lord by then, and I was sure I was supposed to give him up.''

She dashed away angry tears. ''I loved him enough to find what I thought was a good Christian family for him. And then I walked away. But that doesn't mean I did it without a backward glance. Not a day went by that I didn't think of him. Not a day.

''You don't know the depth of my regret after my father died within two years of Jack's birth. My brother contacted me wanting to share Laurel Glen, even though I'd been written out of the will. If I'd known, I'd have held on to my baby—Wade's baby—for all I was worth. I might have found some way to survive those two years and gone home pretending I'd been married to Wade.''

''Fine. You regretted your decision, but why take it out on me?''

''I came to the realization long ago that it was the Lord's will that Jack be raised here in Colorado, but that doesn't mean my anger at you isn't justified. You had the chance to do all the things for him and *with* him that I didn't. That Wade didn't. And you wasted it!''

"You think I don't regret the way things were? That I don't wish I could have those years back? I've accepted that I can't go back. I did my best. I'm sorry you feel my best wasn't good enough, but all we can do is our best. I never had what you did. Family. Constancy. Martha was the light of my life. When she died, my heart just went with her. I told you before that I've made peace with the kids. What right do you have to come here with your feathers ruffled as if I did it to you?''

Meg could see his point. So why couldn't he see hers? "Okay, maybe emotionally you were a mess, but I had a right to expect you to live up to your end of the bargain. I didn't come after him to challenge the adoption when I had other options, did I? If I had, I'd have gotten him—because you broke the contract right off the bat. You didn't name him Wade Jackson Alton. He was supposed to grow up knowing about Laurel Glen. About how Wade died. About how much I loved him. He could have found me years ago."

"The name just felt wrong for him. Jackson suited him. He had the name you wanted, just in a different order. He was supposed to be *our* son, but you wouldn't even let us name him. Even Martha agreed to switch his name. As for the rest, you also didn't want me to give him Martha's heritage. He had to know yours.''

The man was thick as a brick. ''He could have had both! You did none of the things you promised. He only found out about the adoption by accident.''

''There was never a good time to tell him about the adoption. We began to grow apart and I was afraid of his reactions. Besides, I didn't believe all that stuff about you loving him all that much. I thought all the stuff you left behind was for show, to impress that cousin of yours from our church that you were staying with.''

''Why? Why would you think that?''

Evan's blue-gray eyes went cold as chips of ice. ''Because my parents took me to a hospital when I was about six or seven. I was so sick I don't even remember getting there. Then they disappeared. I couldn't be adopted at all because they couldn't even bother signing me over to the state. It wasn't great before, but after that I spent the next nine years practically living as a slave to one farmer or rancher after another. Those people didn't want to be parents to me any more than my own parents did.''

Did he realize how much he'd allowed his parents' actions to direct his attitude toward her? she wondered. ''How did you end up here, then?''

''I ran away from the last place. After that I drifted across the state for about six months doing menial work. I didn't earn much, but at least I was getting paid. Then I came to this place looking for work. I was fifteen or sixteen.''

A terribly sad thought occurred to Meg. ''You don't know exactly how old you are, do you?''

Evan shook his head. ''I always went by the older age approximation the doctors made at the hospital when I was abandoned. My kids don't know that, and I'd appreciate it if you didn't repeat it. It's only a year.''

''No. It's much more. It means your parents never celebrated your birthday. My goodness! It means you made up a birthday.''

''The day I left the last foster home. What's the saying? 'Today is the first day of the rest of your life.'''

''So you and Martha were practically children together. True childhood sweethearts. Losing her must have been like losing half of yourself.''

Evan stared at Meg. How was it the one person on the planet he resented most turned out to be the one person who understood how much of his life had been wrapped up in Martha?

''I can't explain how much losing her changed my world,'' he said finally, knowing he had to break the silence. ''I'd spent more of my life with her than with any other person, including my parents, I think. She was a constant. The voice of my conscience. She led me to the Lord. She taught me what she was learning in school as she went, so I got the education that had been denied to me. She never judged. Never laughed at my lack of manners or table etiquette. She just shot me a look that said, watch me. She had such a gentle heart.''

"Her father didn't mind you two marrying so young?"

"It was his idea. He knew he was dying. I was eighteen when he came to me asking my intentions.'' Evan smiled, remembering that he hadn't had a clue what Frank Waring had been driving at. "I said I thought I'd stay on till he didn't want me there anymore. Happy as I was here, I still wasn't taking anything for granted. I assumed I'd be let go sooner or later. Martha's father just chuckled and said, 'No, knucklehead. I mean are you going to marry my Martha and take over for me when I'm gone?' I was floored. I said something about not thinking I was good enough for her. He handed me a ring that had been in his family and told me to get up to the house and make myself a part of the ranch's future. I handed it back and said if I made myself a part of anything it would be Martha's future.''

Evan shook his head, chuckling at the memory, then he remembered what had followed. "He gave me back the ring and told me he was dying. He didn't have long. Frank said there was no one he trusted with his wife and daughter more than me. He said he knew I loved Martha. I admitted I did, and I made him a promise that day that the ranch would be here for his grandchildren bigger and better than it was then.''

"And I understand you kept that promise." Meg frowned. "Evan, why didn't Jack tell you about me after we met and he heard my reasons for giving him up? Why didn't you ever tell him your reasons for resenting me as a biological parent? You two have to talk to each other. Jack's forgiven you, yes. But I know it was a decision he made while he was at Laurel Glen. Deciding to forgive someone doesn't exactly build a relationship. I, for one, think maybe there's a whole lot less to forgive than either of us thought. Take that chance for you two to become as close as you should be. Tell him all of this. Please.''

Evan sank into the chair at the end of the long table and laced his fingers, resting them on the table-top. He stared at them. Once again, Meg was right. And she wasn't being the least bit arrogant about it. She was giving him advice that could only strengthen his relationship with Jackson. Which meant she didn't want to come between them. Now, there was a surprising truth he'd never even considered. No wonder Jackson still seemed to walk on eggshells around him. Evan was so afraid to lose what he had that he continued to drive it away.

Chapter Six

Evan put Wade into his cradle and went to answer the phone. "Hi," an eastern voice said in greeting. "I wondered if my aunt Meg is there? This is Cole Taggert."

The name Taggert no longer made him tense, and that pleased him. His talk with Meg the day before had allowed him to see his son's birth mother in a new light. He thought they could work together to care for the twins much more easily now.

"I'm sorry, Cole," he told Meg's nephew. "Meg went into Greeley to see Beth. You only missed her by minutes."

"Actually it was Beth I was calling about. How are things going?"

"We're all mighty worried."

"Then she's no better?"

Evan could hear the worry in the voice of Beth's best friend. "I'm sorry the news isn't better, but no, nothing has changed. Maybe you and your wife should visit."

"We'd love to fly out and see her, but CJ isn't doing too good herself right now. She got tossed off a horse earlier in the week, right after Aunt Meg left. She has a pretty bad femur break. I wouldn't feel comfortable leaving her right now, and she's not up to coming there with me."

"Rough luck. I'm sure Beth and Jackson will understand. When I talk to Jackson again, I'll let him know you called."

"Thanks. Tell Aunt Meg about the accident for me, will you? Let her know the doctors are sure CJ will make a full recovery."

Remembering what a talented trainer CJ Taggert seemed to be when he'd met her while on an extended visit to Laurel Glen, Evan said, "I sure will. That must be one mean horse to toss that wife of yours. I'd swear she had superglue on her seat the way she rides."

"Maybe they should rename him Acetone," Cole growled. "Dad already ordered the owner to get him off Laurel Glen."

Evan could understand his actions. Meg's brother, Ross, had lost his first wife when a horse had gone wild, and a teenaged Cole had been watching. He shuddered remembering that in a nearly identical in-

cident both Beth and his daughter, Cris, had nearly
been killed by a dangerously drugged horse. It was
that incident that had taken Evan east to Laurel Glen.

"I'll have your aunt call you when she gets home.
You take it easy and take good care of CJ. I still owe
both of you for stepping in and helping save Cris and
Beth. I'll be sure to pass your get-well wishes on to
Beth, and you do the same with mine to CJ."

After that Evan promised to keep the folks at Laurel Glen up to date on Beth's progress and hung up.
It occurred to him then that Beth's parents had yet to
call. He knew there were hard feelings between her
and her parents over her marriage, but he would have
thought the Boyers would bend now that their daughter was so seriously ill. In fact, he asked Meg about
them and the possibility of their visiting when she
got back later in the day. But Meg just shook her
head as she sat on the sofa facing the fireplace. Evan
sat on the hearth facing her. "I doubt they'll budge
even now. I'll call Beth's brother, Adam, and ask him
if he's contacted them but I don't think it will make
a difference. Jack asked me to call Adam anyway.
He's thinking maybe Adam and his wife, Xandra,
should come. Perhaps you should think of calling
Crystal and Jim, too."

Evan's heart sank. "Beth's that bad that we're
calling the whole family to her side?" He lived every
minute in the fear that his daughter-in-law wouldn't
live. That, Jackson would feel the kind of utter

devastation he had when Martha breathed her last. Though he'd reacted badly to the news that Jackson had decided to stay in Greeley, he was relieved. At least this way Evan didn't have to pretend he thought it would all turn out okay. Because he didn't.

Meg looked as if she was about to cry. "She barely woke up the whole time I was there, and when she did her fever was so high most of what she said made little sense. Jack thought he saw something in her eyes when she saw me, though. Fight, I guess is the best way to describe it. He's hoping if she sees some more familiar faces from back home, it'll help her fight."

"What do the doctors say?"

"That they'll try a new antibiotic tomorrow if she doesn't respond to this one by then."

"But this *was* a new one. I think her OB should have cultured her when what Doc Reynolds put her on didn't work."

Meg sighed. "There's nothing to be gained by speculation. Her OB is off the case anyway. There's an infectious-disease specialist on the case now. And who knows, maybe a visit from her brother will help. And I'm sure Crystal being here would be good for Jackson. I may call Cole, too."

Evan smacked his forehead. "I'm sorry. Your nephew called right after you left this afternoon," he began, and gave Meg the news about CJ. After that Meg called Cole and Adam Boyer, then Evan called

Cris and her husband, Jim Lovell. About dinnertime Cris called back with the news that Jim's sister, who was a pilot, had offered to fly both couples out to Colorado the next day. CJ wasn't up to the trip even in a private plane but she'd insisted Cole come while she spent a few days at Laurel Glen with his father, Ross, and Ross's wife, Amelia. Also staying behind at Laurel Glen was Adam's sixteen-year-old son, Mark.

He and Meg made dinner together, then fed the twins. After tucking Maggie into the bassinet next to Wade's, Evan returned to the living room to rest until the next round of feeding and changing. The fire in the living-room fireplace was blazing cheerfully when he found Meg sitting on the hearth gazing into the leaping flames. Her beauty nearly took his breath away. And when his pulse leaped and his heart began to pound, Evan realized that his reaction to her since they met had been triggered by something he hadn't even felt in years. Something he hadn't recognized.

Attraction.

No wonder he'd been angry when he'd seen her as an enemy. This wasn't something anyone would want to feel for a foe. In a way, he should still be angry with her. The part of himself that felt attraction was supposed to have died with Martha. Yet just looking at Meg Taggert made him feel completely alive once again.

And scared witless!

He told himself it couldn't be. He wouldn't let it be. She was his son's mother and would be in his life on and off for years to come, so he'd better just learn to get a handle on his feelings and deal with them.

"All's quiet on the baby front," he told her as he strode into the room, proud how matter-of-fact he sounded. He flopped as nonchalantly as he could onto the overstuffed sofa, determined to carry on a normal conversation. "Honestly, at the end of a day I feel like a general in the aftermath of a battle. I sit here analyzing how the day went so I can prepare for the new battle. You think that's normal?"

Meg was so lost in thought, she hadn't heard Evan come into the room. She wasn't startled, accustomed as she was to big men who moved like cats. But when she looked away from the fire, her heart stopped for a moment.

Evan Alton was—simply put—a stunning man. As he had said of her, his iron-gray hair was the only thing about him that marked him as being in his fifties. And like her, he was as active as people decades younger. He had what she'd always thought of as a horseman's build. Wide powerful shoulders, a broad chest, slim legs and narrow hips. His blue-gray eyes contrasted with skin tanned by the summer sun. He was devastating to her equilibrium.

And now that the conflict between them had been put to rest, she was hit by an even more devastating thought. This man, this father of her son, made her heart pound as no man since Wade had. And what was more disturbing was that for the first time, Wade's face was nearly impossible to recall.

This couldn't be. She'd spent time around many men before! This was a journey she refused to take.

"I wouldn't have thought it was normal to look at baby-sitting as a campaign, no. Two days ago, that is. But today, General Alton?" She chuckled. "Your second in command thinks it seems perfectly normal. In fact, it smacks of self-preservation. Now I know why the good Lord decided to send children to the very young even though we gain so much more tolerance and patience as we get older," she mused, grinning. But her levity was all a smokescreen to hide the embarrassing fact that she was a bundle of nerves. She felt like a silly schoolgirl with a crush.

It was time to retreat. Regroup.

She pretended to yawn expansively. "Well, I'm turning in early. I suppose I'll see you at two."

Evan grinned, and her stomach turned over. "Or three. Or four. One of these days I expect to wake at dawn and panic. I think Jackson was six weeks old when the sun woke us instead of him. We both went charging into his room expecting to find heaven only knows what. He looked up at us, happy as you please, with an expression on his face that said, 'What is with you two nuts? Can't a guy play alone for a while without causing a big ruckus?' We both saw that look and read the same thing into it. Martha and I nearly fell down, we laughed so hard. He slept through the night every night after that. Kid ate like a pig all day, though.''

"Still does," Meg said. "Jack's appetite has become a legend at Laurel Glen. Thank you for sharing that glimpse into his early life. I'm glad he made you both laugh. When I gave him up I tried to think of it as giving a gift to a couple who wouldn't have gotten the chance to be parents without my sacrifice.'' Meg smiled and stood. She'd really better get out of there before softer emotions broke down her resistance to him.

Evan gazed up at her, looking all the more attractive with the firelight playing on his thick hair and that happy memory still twinkling in his eyes. "You made Martha's last four years happy ones, Meg. It's something I should have thanked you for long ago. And for the record, the doctors said the only reason she was finally able to conceive Cris was that having Jackson around let her relax enough for it to happen. Without you and your sacrifice, we never would have had either of them.''

"I'm glad," Meg said, pasting on a smile to hide her churning emotions. "I'll see you in the morning, be it two or eight.''

Then she retreated, but slumber proved elusive. She lay awake long into the night trying not to think about Evan. When she finally fell into a fitful sleep, the star of her dreams was Evan Alton, not Wade Jackson. It was the first time and, when she woke, she knew with a sinking heart it wouldn't be the last.

Evan insisted Meg be the one to greet the plane at the airstrip near the airport. He said he had more experience handling the twins alone and she couldn't fault his logic. Nor could she pass up the opportunity to put as much space as she could between them. It was a welcome respite.

As she sat across from him eating her breakfast, she'd actually toyed with the idea of renewing hostilities, but she instinctively knew it wouldn't help. And besides, her heart really wasn't in it. Even though her life had been less complicated while they were at odds, she now understood that Evan had had his reasons for viewing her as he did. Plus she could see why he'd been so ill equipped to be a single parent. As he'd said, Jack and Cris had both forgiven him, so who was she to continue a battle declared over by the combatants?

She smiled as she pulled into the front gate of the airstrip Joy Lovell had chosen to use. The military metaphors just kept flowing once Evan had brought up the first one. The smile melted into what her rear-view mirror told her was a stunned expression. It was truly frightening how in tune they were. How much they had in common.

There was their shared love for Jack, Beth and the

twins, of course, but it went beyond that. Both of them were Christians. They both had a love of horses and the great outdoors. And having lost the love of their life decades ago, each continued to hold the precious memories of those two people sacrosanct.

Thankfully she was the only one struck with this ridiculous attraction problem. Only she was bothered that he slept only a few doors away. Meg frowned. Maybe she wasn't so thankful after all! Why should she be the only one suffering? she demanded perversely. Why should she be the only miserable one?

"Because, numbskull, if he felt what you do, one of you might be tempted to do something about it!" she muttered as she got out of the Circle A's big SUV. She'd driven the big vehicle, since she was fetching five adults.

Meg walked into the building. A cheerful woman greeted her and recommended she sit near the window when Meg said she was waiting for someone inbound. Moments later she watched a baby-blue plane dip down out of the fluffy clouds. The little blue dart cut through the sky, circling the field as it lined up for its approach. It landed smoothly and taxied toward the small terminal, where it pulled to a stop with directions from the ground crew.

"You can go out now that the engines have shut down, ma'am."

Meg ground her teeth. She hadn't noticed anyone ever call her ma'am before, but now that she thought about it, it happened all the time. And she hated it. Ever since Evan had pointed out how much her hair color added to her age, she'd been much more aware of clues she'd missed. Maybe she would try to add a little subtle color. There was nothing wrong with looking one's best.

The time for self-examination came to a sudden end as Meg pushed open the door to find that the hatch of the blue plane had swung down into a set of steps. The first one down the stairs was the pilot, Jim Lovell's sister, Joy. Tall and blond like Jim, Joy had the same substantial build as Crystal. She wore an olive flight suit and aviator sunglasses. Jim followed, still the picture of their very own hero cop. When a killer had stalked Crystal, and later Beth, it was Jim who'd unraveled the mystery and stopped the stalker.

The newest of the Laurel Glen newlyweds were next down the steps. Adam Boyer, Beth's older brother, paused to help his wife, Xandra, down the stairs. An ex-navy SEAL, Adam had returned to Pennsylvania with his troubled teenage son, Mark, in time for Beth and Jack's wedding. He'd met Xandra Lexington when she was assigned to be Mark's high school counselor.

Cole was last, after Crystal, and he spotted Meg right away, holding out his arms to her. "How's she doing today, sweetheart?" he asked.

"No better, I'm afraid. It appears to be affecting

her liver and her kidneys. They've decided to change her medication again. She's so weak.''

''How's Jack?''

Tears flooded her eyes as she rested her head against his shoulder. ''Hanging on to hope. He has a hotel room across the street, but I think he sleeps in the chair by her bed.''

''Adam or I will sit with Beth at night instead. We'll make him sleep.''

''That's good. How is CJ?''

''She's fine. I'm a basket case. Truth is, she ordered me to come. Said she was sick of my worried face. Aunt Meg, I'm going to be a mess when she goes back to work.''

''No, you will not! CJ didn't make a peep when you put yourself between Glory and Crystal in that ring. Glory could easily have killed you, and all CJ did was hang back and do what you needed. You can be as nervous a wreck as you want, but you have to show your wife you respect her judgment.''

''Yes, ma'am.''

Ma'am again!

''And speaking of nervous wrecks,'' Cole added, ''we'd better get Adam to the hospital so he can see his sister.''

Chapter Seven

Evan heard the SUV Meg had driven into Greeley rumble by the house and pull into the parking area. He glanced at his watch. Nearly seven o'clock. He'd thought they'd all stay in Greeley until evening visiting hours were over. Evan sighed. So much for a few minutes of uninterrupted downtime now that he'd tucked both babies into their bassinets.

It was no wonder he was tired. He'd gotten almost no sleep the night before thinking about Meg. Then today had turned out to be one of those busy days with the twins. In between dealing with two demanding infants, he'd had to pack up all his things and move back to the cabin, along with making up the guest room.

To be honest, company wasn't the only reason for his move back to the cabin, but it was a plausible one to give them. It probably would have been simpler to give the cabin to one of the couples and Cole, and let the other newlywed couple use Jackson and Beth's room. But now that he was sure the monitor extended as far as the cabin, he'd be sleeping there from now on, putting lots of safe distance between him and Meg.

When he got to the parked SUV, Evan was surprised to find fewer people unloading it than he'd expected. The first person his eyes sought out in the semidarkness was Cris.

She stood alone looking toward the barn, the moonlight bouncing off her ebony hair. Her profile was silhouetted against the bright night sky.

His new son-in-law, Jim, had the habit of calling her his warrior princess. But whatever she looked like, she was his little girl. Evan held out his arms to his beautiful daughter.

"Cris. Honey," he said, and she turned to him, then walked into his embrace. After a long moment he stepped back and continued. "Welcome home. I wish it were under better circumstances. How was Beth today?" He held her by her shoulders, hoping against hope for better news than he'd been hearing for days.

"I think the official word is she's holding her own. Jackson's nearly destroyed, Dad." Cris's slightly alto voice shook.

"I know. He's a mess. I tried to tell him ruining

his own health wouldn't help Beth, he's not listening.'' He grimaced. ''Some things never change, I guess.''

''He does look awful, but try not to worry. Adam and Cole stayed behind to spell him at the hospital. They said they'd hog-tie him if that's what it took to get him to sleep.'' She smiled. ''I don't think either of them have a clue what hog-tying is, but they seemed more than willing to try.''

''City boys,'' Evan teased, to lighten the mood. That phrase could also apply to Jim, who was pulling the luggage out of the back of the SUV.

''Yes, but Adam was a navy SEAL. He probably has innumerable ways to subdue Jack,'' said a woman on the other side of the SUV he didn't know. She was medium height with wavy dark hair. He assumed she was married to Beth's brother. She smiled and held out her hand. ''Hi. I'm Alexandra Boyer.''

''Good to meet you,'' Evan said as he took her hand. He still marveled at the marriage of Beth's brother to the sister of the teen who'd brutally raped Beth when she was fourteen.

Poor Beth. She hadn't yet recovered when Jackson had met her years later at Laurel Glen. But the Lord and meeting Jackson had helped her finally heal. It didn't seem fair that she should be struggling for life when her life had, in many ways, only just begun.

''Only you would call someone who grew up at Laurel Glen a 'city boy,''' Meg drawled as she finally came around the luggage from the far side of the car. "And Adam grew up next door. He and Beth were on horseback before they could ride a tricycle."

"Yeah, and I protest that city-boy reference, too, Evan," Jim protested with a laugh. "I'm city born and bred, but I learned to hog-tie with the best of them."

Evan grinned. "Only if someone else did the roping. I won't soon forget you trying to lasso calves on that roundup. Kept us all entertained for the whole two weeks. Most fun any of us have had on a roundup in years."

"So Cole and Adam stayed behind in Greeley to be near Beth," he repeated, trying to mentally shuffle guest rooms.

Cris and Meg nodded and Jim said, "Which leaves you and me to tote and carry, Evan. Did you put Crystal and me in the cabin?"

Evan shook his head as he walked to the pile of luggage. Why did easterners travel so heavy? He picked up a couple of bags and led the way up the walk. Rather than go around to the formal entrance at the front of the house, he led them in through what he'd always thought of as the family entrance. Because Jackson and Cris had married, the definition of family had grown. He found, quite to his surprise, that he no longer minded the inclusion of the Taggerts.

Everyone made themselves comfortable around the

big table and he handed out hot coffee as Cris prepared tea for Xandra. ''I'd been thinking Jim and I would stay in the cabin,'' Cris said when she settled next to her husband on the bench. Jim, almost as if it were an unconscious movement, wrapped his arm around her waist.

Evan had to look away. They were so happy. What would Cris do if something happened to Jim? He was a cop, after all. He just couldn't stand the thought of his kids feeling the kind of soul wrenching pain he had.

He turned his gaze back to Cris. ''I moved back out to the cabin this afternoon, honey. I'll still hear the twins in the middle of the night, so you don't have to worry about that. The monitor works even beyond that distance, and this way you can all be in the main house with a well-stocked kitchen. Mine's empty of staples right now, since I've been staying in the house.''

''Dad, you didn't need to do that.''

Oh, yes, I did, he thought, but said, ''It wasn't any trouble.''

Cris grinned. ''Well, good, because this'll work out even better. Until Joy comes back to get us at the end of next weekend, the five of us are taking turns with the babies, and you and Meg are to rest and relax in between visits with Beth.''

Evan looked at Jim. A police detective, a navy SEAL, a veterinarian and two women who, as far as he knew, had no experience whatsoever with babies? He didn't think so.

His feelings must have shown on his face. "Before you get all protective, Adam helped out a lot with his son when he was a baby, Jim baby-sits all the time for scads of friends and Cole has had lots of practice for two years now with his little sister, Laurel, and his niece."

"Close your mouth, Evan, dear. You'll catch flies," Meg cracked from the other end of the table.

Meg. She was the big problem with this, too. They might expect him to entertain her. Maybe even go to the hospital together. He didn't see how he could do either. Now what?

"Have you seen much of the ranch, Meg?" Jim asked, starting that first dreaded ball rolling.

"I've been helping Evan with Wade and Maggie or going to and from the hospital since I arrived. There hasn't been time. Wait till you try juggling those two sleeping angels upstairs."

"It'll be good practice. And the weather forecast for tomorrow is perfect for a ride," Cris said. "Sunny skies and seventy. Jackson mentioned that Glory's probably about kicking down her stall."

That was too true. The Irish Draught *was* getting antsy. She missed the attention she usually got from both Beth and Jackson. Since Beth's advanced pregnancy had stopped her from riding before she even arrived in Colorado, Jackson had taken Glory out for exercise every couple of days, but Jackson, like Evan and every other sane man on the ranch, didn't ride English tack or fly horses over fences. It would be selfish to deny the animal the kind of exercise she was used to.

He'd seen Meg ride, and it was truly like watching water flow. Smooth and fluid with a kind of mastery over the animal, like working a quarter horse, she displayed partnership and dominion in one package.

In short, it, no, *Meg,* had been beautiful.

Meg watched Evan's expression mutate into a scowl. "I can't believe you flew thousands of miles to baby-sit. I'll watch the babies and you show Meg around, then, honey," Evan said. "You probably haven't had the chance to ride flat-out for months."

Thank heavens. It was clear from his reaction that he wasn't feeling the attraction she was. Unless he's blocking it, just like you, a pesky voice in her head added.

"Oh, no, you don't!" Crystal said. "I'm not letting you bury yourself in yet another kind of work. Jackson told me how much help you've been since Beth got sick. He says you ought to be about ready to drop. I'll remind you of what you said to Jackson. 'You won't do the twins any good if you harm your own health.' We'll be gone in a little over a week, Dad. Take advantage of the rest while you can. Okay?"

Evan held up his hands. "Okay. Okay." He glanced at Meg, and his direct gaze made her want to squirm. "I surrender."

And that was how Meg found herself mounted on Glory and following Evan out of the corral the next morning. He sat so straight in the saddle. A true horseman, even though according to Jack he was considered a cattleman.

"I always thought of Colorado as being cold in winter," she said, finding Evan's silence unnerving. She glanced at his handsome face. His blue-gray eyes seemed to sparkle even in the shade of his hat.

"Colorado's dry and changeable. In a few days we could drop down to zero. Or a blizzard could roar across the plains and dump a foot of snow. Then it could warm up again and melt just as fast." He looked away, then pointed to a fence. "Think you can jump that fence with her? Glory hasn't been given her particular type of workout since she got here."

Meg nodded and urged Glory into a canter. "Race you," she called over her shoulder. She could hear Evan's Apple Boy thundering after her, but the fence was there. She knew she'd won as Glory took flight and they sailed through the air, weightless just for a moment at the top of the arc. Then they landed and she turned back to watch Evan's quarter horse ride the fence line to an opening, practically turn on a dime and race back to her.

Evan rode up to her, grinning. As he came to a stop, he leaned on the pommel, so relaxed in the saddle he looked as if he'd been born there. He shook his head.

"Poetry in motion. And insane."

She laughed. "You act as if you've never seen someone jump over a barrier. I've seen Jack jump streams and fallen trees as shortcuts."

"None of which are four feet high."

She tilted her head. "How do you feel about Jack changing the focus of the ranch?"

Evan shrugged. "That he's probably right. Diversification. A big word for a smart idea. Cris has been saying it for years about investments. I listened because I knew nothing about finance and she went to school for it. I wanted my kids to have a good education. It was something I wanted, but never had the chance to get formally. Not just for education's sake, but for something to use. Jackson felt differently. We disagreed on his major in college. Not the first disagreement we've had or the last, of course. He took some courses related to ranching, but he was always interested in history. He got his master's in it. I thought it was a waste of time. So when he said we should diversify the Circle A, I dug my heels in. Too stubborn to bend. Times had changed, but I didn't want to. I'd built the place on cattle. Seemed to me at the time we could keep it running on cattle. But he's right. That market's shrinking. The quarter horse market isn't. Not with Jackson training them, at least. The Circle A will be fine. You have to see him work Duke. Pure magic. He may have done a bang-up job as foreman for both the Circle A and Laurel Glen, but he was wasted in the position."

"Duke? Isn't that the horse who kept dragging Jim off his feet when Crystal was teaching him to ride? That didn't sound well trained to me."

"You ever seen any quarter horse work?"

"I don't think so. I once saw a video of a barrel race."

"That's rodeo stuff. See those cows over there?" Evan asked, pointing down the hill. "Cows like to stay together, but watch me cut two away from the others. Jackson trained Apple Boy, too."

Meg's heart was warmed by the pride Evan took in Jack. It was a side of him she not only hadn't seen, but one she hadn't known existed. As she watched the performance of Evan and his quarter horse the pounding of her heart worried her. It had nothing to do with trepidation for Evan's safety or excitement over the impressive display of talent, however. It was due to one reason and one reason only. He looked… attractive in the saddle. There, she'd said it. Evan Alton was a desirable man and she was suddenly scared to death to be near him.

And there was nowhere to run.

Chapter Eight

As she watched Evan finish cutting the cows away from the herd, Meg knew she had to get a grip on her runaway response to him. But she couldn't keep resorting to rudeness to keep those feelings at bay. It would be wrong, especially after he'd swallowed his pride and shared with her the tragedy of his early life and the reason he'd been so ill equipped to bring up his children without Martha.

Who was she to judge him, after all? She'd spent years living in a state of solitary grief, working just as hard in her career as he had on the ranch. Her life had turned around only because her brother had called to tell her his wife, Marley, had been killed. When she'd gone home for the funeral, the deep grief in Cole's eyes, as well as the hollow look of loss in his sister Hope's, had cried out to her. She'd stayed to help them, but they had helped her just as much.

Ross's children had given her a new purpose and a chance to mother someone. A chance to be part of a family again.

But she'd had family in her formative years. Evan had had no such experience to miss. Or aspire to. It was no small wonder that, in his grief, he hadn't missed what he'd never had.

She also couldn't take her fear out on him. And she *was* afraid of the things he made her feel. Because Wade Jackson had been a careless, reckless youth in comparison to the man riding toward her. Even in his teens, Evan wouldn't have left her alone and pregnant, Meg could tell. The ring he'd have placed on her finger wouldn't have been a promise of a future he might not have, but would have been a wedding ring that would have protected her both socially and financially when he went off to war.

She hadn't missed the significance of Evan's father-in-law having placed his daughter's heart and future in Evan's hands at such a young age. It was also clear that, though Evan had loved Martha from afar, he'd held her in too high a regard to consider himself good enough for her. It hurt to realize that Wade had not had that same esteem for Meg.

She shook her head. No, there was no sense going there. She couldn't start second-guessing their love and its result. And she could not wish it hadn't happened, or she'd be wishing her wonderful son out of existence.

She was, however, sorry she'd broken God's law. As usual, the Lord in His goodness had taken her regrettable choice and made of it something wonderful. Even though she'd had to go through years of pain to find the prize at the end of that long road her love for Wade had started her on, she was thankful, because Jack was in her life.

"And that's what a cutting horse does," Evan said, breaking her train of thought as he and his horse stopped on a dime in front of her.

"There's a good market for them, you say?"

"Seems to be."

She forced a smile, refusing to show the path her mind had taken. "Then good for Jack that he saw it. I think I'm going to have to learn that kind of riding. It looked like fun."

Evan could feel Meg's restlessness as they trotted along next to each other. They'd ridden out to Half-Pint Spring, where they talked for a spell about their lives. He'd told her about the changes he'd made to the Circle A and about the careful land purchases he'd made to expand it. She had explained that her brother had done the same thing with Laurel Glen, through an inheritance of a neighboring estate when his first wife died and the recent purchase of some land from Adam Boyer.

And now they rode on to Aspen Stand, one of the northernmost man-made watering holes, so she could see a windmill in action. He glanced at her. Was she as nervous as she seemed? Why was that? Did she sense his unruly feelings?

No. No way. He was better at hiding things than that. Besides, he'd been a quarter of a mile away earlier and had returned to find these vibes. So what was wrong? Maybe it was knowing they were out of touch with how Beth was doing. Well, of course that was it! Hadn't she said Beth was like the daughter she'd never had? This ride had probably been torture for her.

"Maybe we should get back." He checked Apple Boy and they stopped. Meg wheeled Glory to face him after a few paces. Evan looked at the position of the sun, then reached for his watch to confirm the startling fact that they'd been riding for over two hours. Time had simply taken wing. "You can still make afternoon visiting hours if we head in now. Would you like that?"

She seemed to grasp eagerly at the suggestion. "I would, yes. I'm so worried about her. And Jack."

Meg looked so concerned Evan felt like a fool. Some leisurely ride. He sidestepped Apple Boy. "I'm sorry. If you'd wanted to skip the tour you should have just said."

She looked startled. "No. I had a nice time. Really."

He shrugged and started them for home. Halfway there Evan realized Meg might think he intended to go to the hospital with her. That wasn't going to happen. He knew with a certainty that if he went near that hospital Beth wouldn't live to see the twins again. Just as Martha hadn't lived to see her children grow up. It made no sense. He was as certain that it made no sense as he was that he couldn't go there.

He pulled up when the ranch compound came into view. "You can get there without me along from here. Tell Tomas to take care of Glory. I have to check out something in the western part of our land. I'll see you later." He tipped his hat, pivoted Apple Boy off to the left and kicked him into a canter.

He rode hard for a good hour before returning to the compound, then he showered and kicked back to watch some TV. Except, nothing held his attention. He paced awhile then flipped through the channels again. Bored. He was bored, he told himself. So he fired up the computer and did a little stock trading, adjusting his portfolio. Checked for e-mail messages. Other than a bunch of spam, there was nothing.

Still restless, he decided to walk down to the corral and see if anything was up down there. He found Cris instead, her raven's-wing hair hanging loose down her back. "Honey, I thought you'd go with Meg."

Cris turned to him. She wore a pair of tan slacks and a soft red turtleneck sweater. She dressed differently now. No men's shirts tucked into jeans. There was an air of sophistication and polish about her these days that made her seem all grown up for the first time.

"Xandra went instead," she told him. "She and Beth have a special bond. I guess I should explain so you don't say the wrong thing. Dad, Beth helped rescue Xandra from an abusive marriage by taking her into the women's shelter she founded. Xandra took over New Life Inn for Beth when they came here. She lived at the shelter until she married Adam."

Shaking his head in rueful sorrow, Evan said, "You think it only happens in the inner city or among the poor. Not to people with money. And speaking of people with money, I thought Alexandra had parents who could have helped her get away."

"They thought just like you said. That abuse doesn't happen at their income level. Or in a beautiful house. Thank God she had the strength to get out. Every time I think about what Xandra went through, I automatically think of the Harts and how Josiah Hart killed his wife in front of Caleb and his sister. If only Mrs. Hart had found the strength to get away the way Xandra did."

Evan grimaced, remembering as if it were yesterday the day two decades ago when news of the murder had flashed through town. "Short of that, the law should have intervened," Evan growled. He felt a little guilty. If he hadn't been so preoccupied with himself, maybe he would have seen what was happening on a neighboring ranch. Maybe he could have helped.

"Sheriff Barrett stepped in and straightened Caleb out when he kept getting into trouble in his teens. I don't think that would have been possible if Caleb had thought the sheriff could have done more. But I do think Caleb is still pretty bitter about his mom. If he only knew the Lord, maybe he could get past all that." She sighed. "So, how is Caleb doing still working for the worst sheriff Torrence, Colorado, has ever elected?"

"Caleb's always done a good job, but people can't seem to see past the trouble he got into in his teens. I knew it was bound to happen. I feel bad that Caleb lost the election, but now the town's at risk. That's why I tried to talk Jim into running."

"You mean it wasn't just so your little girl wouldn't move away?" Cris asked, then sighed. "I really like Caleb. I hate to see him banging his head against a wall like this. He should have just moved away, both from the town and his past."

Evan winced, understanding Caleb more than anyone did. "He wants to prove himself. I understand it. I also know he's wasting his time. Not that he won't do it eventually, but by then he'll have wasted a lot of years."

Cris's gaze sharpened and she propped a hand on her hip. "Are we talking about Caleb Hart or Evan Alton now?"

Smart girl. A year ago he'd have denied it. "Both. I told Meg I'd think about telling you and Jackson about my early life. It seems you know more than I thought."

"Grandmother thought if we knew you'd had no family and grew up in foster care that we'd understand your lack of affection. That's about all I know. You came here as a runaway at sixteen and never left."

Evan nodded and gazed out over the beautiful world his in-laws had opened up to him. It was easier to say that way. He didn't want to see pity on his daughter's face, but he knew Meg was right. They had a right to know. It had affected their lives, too. And if his story helped them understand him more, so much the better.

"There's a little more to it than that. I never told Mary all of it. My parents abandoned me sick at a hospital when I was about six or seven. The age was a guesstimate, kiddo. I didn't even know my birthday. Frank, Mary and Martha were my salvation in more ways than just showing me the way to the Lord. I'm sorry I didn't learn more from them about how to make us a family."

He looked at her then and her eyes sparkled with unshed tears. She flung herself against him. "Oh, Daddy. I'm so sorry." She snuffled and backed away, her gaze fierce, her tears clumping her long lashes into spikes. "Oh, treating a child like that! What is wrong with some people?"

"Cris, calm down, honey. Even I'm not this angry. I made too many mistakes with you and Jackson to hold them in contempt."

She wiped her eyes. "Oh, don't mind me. It's the hormones." Her eyes widened. "Oops."

Evan felt his mouth stretch into a wide smile even as he was processing what she'd let slip. "Do you and my son-in-law have an announcement?"

Her hand went to her still-flat stomach. "We were going to wait till Beth's better. I didn't know how you'd take it, considering."

He held out his arms. "I'm thrilled, honey. My only regret is that my grandchild will live across the country."

She shot him a dark look. "Dad, don't start the 'moving home' stuff again."

Evan held up his hand, still grinning like an idiot. "I'm not. I know you love it there. Now, come give Daddy a hug." She did, and they started back toward the house.

"You've flourished and blossomed there, Cris. I'd have to be blind not to see it. I don't know if it has anything to do with the location, other than that's where Jim hails from, but you look wonderful and happy, honey. So are we going to be surprised or do we know if this is a grandson or granddaughter? You get to break the tie, you know."

"It's a girl. Oh, Daddy, can't you just see Jim with a girl?"

Evan chuckled. "She'll wrap him around her little finger. But I can also see him standing on your front porch with his arms crossed, staring daggers at her dates, too. Poor little girl. She's doomed to be an old maid. Then again, if she's as pretty as her mother, they'll beat a path to her door in spite of him."

"Funny, I don't remember any path-beating around here."

"That's because the locals were blind, as Jim says every time the subject comes up. Man seems mighty grateful they were, for all his grousing about it."

A slight blush tinged her cheeks. "We…uh…we already decided on a name."

He steeled himself. But it wasn't necessary.

"Martha Mary," she said, and shot him a grin. "At first Jim thought that was too many *m*'s, but then he thought we could call her Em or Emmy. Kind of cute, huh?"

Now Evan was the one fighting tears. He slung his arm over Cris's shoulders and pulled her against his side and they walked to the house in step.

"Thank you, honey," he said. "I understood Jackson and Beth's reasons for naming the twins what they did, but Martha had such a short life. It's nice to see her name carried into the next generation."

"I wish I could remember her. I always thought I did, but I've only begun to realize that it's the stories about her I remember. I even thought I remembered her smell, but when I was packing up my things to move east, I came across some of her things and realized it was a sachet someone had put in the trunk of her clothes that I'd smelled over the years when I peeked in there. I was too young to remember that, wasn't I?''

Evan grimaced. But for the first time the stinging pain he'd been ready for wasn't there. ''I'm afraid so, Cris. But she loved you very much. Both you and Jackson. I like to think you carry that with you, even if you don't remember how you know.''

She smiled sadly. ''I do, too, Dad. She must have been something if you still miss her so much after all these years.''

''Yeah,'' he said, his voice sounding wistful but not agonized, even to himself. No, he'd never forget her, but a niggling voice in his head told him she'd have wanted him to go on and live a fuller life than he had been.

Unfortunately, he just couldn't leave her behind. His love for her was too comfortable. Too much a part of him.

Chapter Nine

Meg returned from the hospital just in time to wash up and carry a big soup tureen full of Xandra's hearty chili to the table. She set it next to a basket of fry bread Crystal had whipped up. Everyone gathered around the table and automatically joined hands to pray as soon as she sat—all but Evan. He missed a beat, then looking terribly self-conscious, finally reached out for her hand and Xandra's. When Evan remained silent, not taking the lead in prayer as the head of the household, Cole smoothly stepped in and began to pray over the meal, almost covering the awkward moment.

Unfortunately, Evan's touch distracted Meg so much she didn't have a clue what her nephew said. All she could think about was the way Evan's hand engulfed hers, the feel of his work-roughened palm against her knuckles. Its strength. Its warmth.

"So how was Beth today?" Jim asked, bringing her out of her thoughts. Meg's gaze flew to Evan's. He was still holding her hand. She stared into his eyes, unable to look away for a prolonged moment. When Cole cleared his throat, Evan blinked and let go of her hand, as if coming out of a trance. He looked down at his plate, but she continued to stare at the top of his head.

"I'd say about the same," Cole answered Jim, ignoring them. "She spiked another high fever about the time Aunt Meg got there."

Hearing her name finally pulled Meg back to the conversation and she managed to add, "Jack was beside himself."

But as if drawn by some invisible force, Meg glanced at Evan just as he looked back up, confusion and worry warring in his gaze. "He'd had such high hopes for this new antibiotic," he said, his voice sounding husky and strained.

Was he worried about Beth? Or because of that... that moment they might or might not have shared? She prayed her own quick prayer for support, then forced her mind back to the purpose of her visit to Colorado.

"He did have high hopes. Her doctor hasn't given up on it, but he did say he had something stronger waiting in the wings. We prayed together and that seemed to settle them both down. Jack always takes comfort in his faith, and it seemed to ease Beth so she could rest.''

"Has he been letting you spell him, Cole?'' Evan asked.

"He got about six hours' sleep last night and looked a lot better for it.'' Cole grimaced. "At least until Beth's fever spiked.''

"I got permission to take the babies in to see her,'' Meg told Evan. "We're hoping seeing them will raise her spirits. Could you make the trip with me tomorrow?''

Evan frowned and quickly shook his head. "Can't... I...uh...I have a meeting in Denver first thing Monday. I was going to change my plans but when all these guys flew out I realized I didn't need to. I'd planned to leave right after church tomorrow and stay overnight at a friend's house. Maybe Crystal and Jim could help. It'd be good practice for them.''

"We'd be glad to,'' Crystal said. "I'd hoped to go see Beth tomorrow anyway.''

"Is it safe for the babies to be near her?'' Evan wondered, his concern clear on his face. At first Meg was relieved that all they shared was a mutual love for Jack, Beth and the babies, but something sharp and aware in his expression nagged at her. She shook it off and replied, "The doctor said it's perfectly safe to take them in.''

Cole cleared his throat, and she realized that once again her attention had been so ensnared by Evan that she had ignored the others. She glanced at Cole and found her nephew staring at her, his gaze both curious and speculative. Then he winked and she knew just what he was thinking—what he'd seen. Dismayed by the telltale blush she felt heat her cheeks, she decided any protest would open up a conversation she wanted to avoid at all costs.

So she steered the conversation to the honeymoon trip Crystal and Jim had taken, and the topic stuck on travel for a while. She told them about her past travels and had them all laughing about one trip she'd taken on the spur of the moment. It had been during a very uncomfortable period when Cole first returned to live at Laurel Glen after years away. Cole and Ross had been engaged in a father-son war that had her itching to throttle both of them. She'd taken the expression "take the high road" literally and had simply left!

Cole teased her about a few other spontaneous trips she'd taken over the years, accusing her of deserting a sinking ship. She teased him right back, saying if that were so, then he'd often been the torpedo.

She should have known Cole wouldn't be that easily put off by her change of topic, even though he'd gone along with it. He'd inherited a full measure of Taggert tenacity. She was sure she'd escaped until she was just about finished cleaning up the kitchen.

As she rinsed the sink, Cole's arms stole around her waist from behind and he wrapped her in a bear hug.

"Am I about to lose my favorite aunt to the wilds of Colorado?" he whispered, then stepped back, allowing her to dry her hands and turn to face him. As she did, he hitched his hip onto the sturdy trestle table behind him and crossed his arms. "Do I need to ask Evan Alton his intentions?" he asked, a teasing light in his eyes belying his frown.

"What on earth are you talking about?" She, too, crossed her arms, leaning back against the sink.

"Come off it. We all saw the way you and Evan looked at each other. No, make that couldn't take your eyes off each other. When you weren't sending little glances in his direction, he was sneaking peeks at you. What gives?"

"Are you talking about romance?" she demanded, deciding to play dumb after all. What did she have to lose? He grinned slowly in answer. She might be busted, but she wasn't going down without a fight. "Between Evan and me? Well, get that out of your foolish head right now. Goodness, can't two people share a…a concern for their child without it having overtones of…of…" Words failed her.

"Attraction? Interest? Happily ever after?" His grin widened.

"Foolishness? Disaster? Heartache?" she countered. "I've been down that road, Cole. I have no *desire* to go there again. I've yet to recover from the first time.''

"First time? Is there a second?" he asked, his gaze sharpening. "Come on, Meg. Evan's a good-looking guy. And a good man. Why let ancient history stand in your way? You have nearly half your life yet to live. Do you really want to live it alone?"

"I am not alone! My life is more full of loved ones now than ever. I don't need a man to worry about. I have Jack and Beth and the twins. I have Ross and Amelia and their children. Hope, Jeff and theirs. You and CJ and any children you two have. And what was that grimace about?" What a perfect opportunity to change the subject. "Is there a problem we need to hash out?"

"Don't go trying to change the subject. We were talking about you."

"We have. The subject is now closed. In fact, there was no subject in the first place. Now, sit! What is going on between you and CJ? I knew you were driving her crazy after she was hurt, but is there more to it than that?"

Cole sat, his broad shoulders slumping a bit. "I guess I said some stupid things after the accident. I think I'm messing this marriage up." There was real fear in his voice. "I love her so much. I can't lose her."

Meg sat across from him. She'd seen this coming even before the wedding, but she'd hoped he'd see what he was doing. "Are you still trying to make things fit that mythical fairy tale you see as the perfect life for CJ? I'm afraid it may be coming off as if you're trying to remake her."

His chocolate eyes widened. "Oh-oh. That's an awful lot like what she said. What am I doing that's so wrong?"

"Trying too hard. Not listening to her real wishes. You insisted on a long courtship and a big wedding when CJ would just as soon have knocked on Jim Dillon's door and been married in his kitchen."

"I wanted her to have all the stuff she'd done without all those years. What's wrong with that?"

"Nothing, if those were the things she'd wanted. I went along because she was willing and I honestly thought she might look back with regret on a small affair. Shopping for that dress and trousseau was sheer torture for her, but I thought the wedding and extended honeymoon would be the end of it as far as you were concerned. I thought it had been. Now, what happened that she sent you here when she should have wanted you with her?"

He hesitated. "She wanted to have a baby."

Meg's eyes widened. "And you don't?"

"I wanted her to quit first, but—"

"Quit working at Laurel Glen?" That made no sense at first, then light dawned. His mother's death. "Oh, Cole, what did you say?"

Cole just shrugged. "That I didn't want the mother

of my children killed like—'' he began, then she watched as horror dawned on her nephew's face.

She held up her hand. ''Never mind. I think my imagination will fill in the rest. You march yourself upstairs and pack. I'll call the airlines and book a flight home for you. You can ride into Denver with Evan. Then you go home and crawl to her. You tell CJ you love her just as she is. You tell her your children will be lucky to have a mother as talented as she is. And you make it clear that she can keep her job if she wants, and have as many babies as she wants at the same time.''

''She could die and leave us all alone.'' Cole all but cried.

''Like your mother did.'' Meg paused and let that bald fact speak for itself. ''You know Ross is nearly pathological about the safety of the animals CJ trains at Laurel Glen. Yes, accidents do happen. And, yes, one dangerous horse slipped through the cracks recently and CJ was hurt. I imagine the new foreman is looking for a job about now?''

Cole nodded.

''Cole, Beth could die tonight. Right now. Of *sickness*. None of us knows how long we have on this earth. You have to put what happened to your mother behind you once and for all. The Lord put you and CJ together to have a future. Not to relive the past. He wants you to live. To love. To flourish. Now, go home and do all three and stop looking back!''

Cole nodded and smiled sadly. "I guess I should have talked to you before." He turned to go, but stopped and pivoted back. "You know that passage from the New Testament? I think it's toward the beginning of Matthew 7? Jesus asks why we see the speck in our brother's eye, but don't seem to notice the plank in our own. Take your own advice, sweetheart. Live. Love. Be happy. You deserve it more than anyone I know." He winked and was gone.

Meg stared at his retreating back. The little sneak. He'd really nailed her with that one. She shook her head and stood. Her thoughts were in too much of a turmoil to do any good just then. Instead she went looking for a phone book.

She didn't have time for foolish introspection about impossibilities. Evan was her complete opposite. He'd spent years avoiding loved ones. She'd spent her life embracing them and helping them weather crises. He was so entrenched on the ranch that he wouldn't even consider traveling to visit Crystal and Jim to watch his grandchildren grow. She loved travel and adventure.

No, she and Evan were polar opposites. And she didn't want a man anyway. Been there. Done that. Burned her commemorative T-shirt long ago.

Chapter Ten

Evan sat in his cabin staring into the flames of the fireplace. He'd been unsettled since he'd left Dr. Campbell's office the day before, more troubled than when he went in. For the second session in a row she'd talked about his recovery in such worldly terms that he'd begun to feel uncomfortable. Jackson had said all along that he should seek out a Christian counselor, and Evan was now sure his son was right. He and his psychiatrist were further apart than he'd thought.

Since Meg had arrived, he'd noticed the way she and all the visiting easterners relied on their faith on a daily basis. He'd tried to pray for Beth. Had prayed. But he had a hard time believing God would honor his prayers, because he didn't really believe God would heal her. He hadn't spared Martha. Why would He spare Beth?

It was a real reminder of how far he'd drifted from the man he'd been when he'd had Martha and her parents in his life. In fact, while listening to Dr. Campbell go on and on with her cynical view of where he needed to go next in his life, he'd realized Martha might not have agreed to marry the man he was today. It was a real wake-up call.

His psychiatrist thought he should start dating again, but she didn't seem to be able to grasp his point of view on dating in general. She thought he was making excuses, because she saw dating as an end in itself. A no-strings exercise that led to mutual satisfaction for both parties. He saw dating as a beginning that signaled a desire to explore the future commitment of marriage. He wasn't ready for that kind of step. He wasn't sure he ever wanted to be. Because he never wanted to feel the loss of a life partner again.

Martha was the only woman he'd ever dated, and that was with marriage in mind from that first town dance he'd taken her to. They'd known each other well by then and he'd been courting her as his future wife. Courting was an old-fashioned word and concept, but it was the one that fit. Maybe it wasn't so much old-fashioned as small-town. Dating, to him, was a time of getting to know someone you were already nearly sure you wanted to marry.

Meg's face popped into his mind, shocking Evan.

Why had it not been Martha he'd seen in his mind's eye?

"Because Martha's your past," he said aloud. And he knew it was true.

But that didn't mean Meg was his future, his mind protested. It couldn't. There wasn't going to be a wife in his future. He'd admit he was aware of her as he had been of no other woman in nearly thirty years. Meg was a striking woman. It was no small wonder he'd noticed her. Especially with her practically living under his roof.

Two nights ago at dinner was a prime example. He knew she'd thought his delay in joining hands at dinner was an unfamiliarity with prayer at the table, but that wasn't the case. It was a very real reluctance to touch her. One split second of having her soft hand in his and his mind had short-circuited. But it was clear she didn't share his problem.

Thank heaven for small favors.

Evan heard a knock on the cabin door. He glanced at the clock on the mantel. It was ten o'clock in the morning. Praying it wasn't bad news, he went to the door. It was ironic, given his earlier thoughts, that it was Meg on his doorstep. She'd steered clear of the cabin. She looked as if she were dressed to go into Greeley again. Soft-looking pastel wool slacks hugged her hips and a matching silky-looking shirt the same pale blue color topped off the outfit.

"Meg! Is something wrong?" he asked.

She shook her head.

"Oh. Good. Then what can I do for you?"

"You can start by inviting me in," she told him, her voice sharply reminiscent of her first days there.

He didn't want visions of her in the cabin in his mind, but saw no choice but to acquiesce. He gestured toward the living-room area. She was clearly annoyed. What had he done to put a burr under her saddle? He stirred up the fire, then realized he was only putting off the inevitable confrontation. Settling in the chair across from the sofa where she sat, he asked, "What's on your mind?"

"I want to know why you didn't go to the hospital on your way past Greeley yesterday."

Evan stilled. Oh. She'd noticed. He'd hoped staying away from the main house all day and night would help him dodge that particular question. "I'm not much for hospitals," he replied flatly. He wasn't ready to get into this, but he wouldn't lie either.

"I wasn't sure until I talked to Jack a little while ago, but he confirmed what I suspected. You haven't been to see Beth even once."

He shrugged, trying for nonchalance. When her eyes widened and her nostrils flared, Evan realized his error. He'd been without a woman in his life too long to handle these things on the fly. It had been his problem with Cris. Invariably his first inclinations were okay on Mars but a disaster on Venus.

"You say you want a good relationship with Jack,

but you can't even be bothered to go see his wife—his precariously ill wife. How can you treat them this way?''

He stood. If the best defense was a good offense, then he was in trouble, because he didn't have one. She was right. So he borrowed another tried-and-true battle plan—he who runs away lives to fight another day.

''I don't want to talk about it,'' he grated, and stalked to the door. Grabbing his jacket and hat as he passed the clothes tree, he headed for the barn under a full head of steam. She'd have a time of it negotiating the cracked stone of the drive in her soft-soled shoes, and that would give him all the time he needed.

He heard her shouting after him as he rode bare-back out of the yard. It had been years since he'd ridden off in the face of problems. The last time was the day Frank Waring died, leaving Evan to carry on with the ranch at barely nineteen, just weeks before his wedding to Martha. He'd been tempted to keep on riding then, riding right into the sunset. He felt the same way today. But his promise to Frank had weighed on him then as well as his love for Martha, and he'd turned around, taking on what had felt to his young shoulders like the weight of the world. He'd kept his promise to Frank, but there was still the one he'd made to Martha. The one he'd spent years breaking and was breaking once again.

He should be there at Northern Colorado Medical, supporting Jackson. But he couldn't—he just couldn't—go to that hospital and watch his son experience the same nightmare he had. History was repeating itself, but this time there'd be no Mary Waring to help raise a boy and a girl. Was Jackson any more equipped to handle that than Evan had been?

He slowed at Half-Pint Springs and dismounted. Apple Boy, his sides heaving, nuzzled him, making Evan feel a second weight of guilt. Grabbing the quarter horse by the halter, Evan walked him for a while to cool him down, then tore up clumps of grass and rubbed the lathered animal down with them. After what felt like the right amount of time, he let Apple Boy have a drink before turning him loose to do a little wandering. At that point Evan didn't care if the quarter horse wandered all the way back to the compound. Being stranded would give him that much longer to get a handle on his feelings.

With the innocent animal cared for, Evan sank onto a rock. As he looked out over the lonely plains, the nearby rippling water, he felt a bit calmer. He glanced up, letting the sunshine hit his face. The sun hung like a ball of fire in the sky, but in spite of the warmth of the day, it was apparent to Evan that winter would soon return with a vengeance. Fluffy clouds swept across the blue horizon like windblown cotton. Oh, yeah. There'd be snow and subzero temperatures within a day. It was easy to read the signs after seeing them all these years.

Evan wished signs of other impending calamities were as easy to read. If they were, he might have walked on by the Warings' place that day. Barring that, he'd have told Jackson of his adoption so he'd never have gone in search of Meg Taggert and Laurel Glen. His son would never have met Elizabeth Boyer and wouldn't be glued to her side right now as she struggled for life.

He sat for a long time, staring out across the water, as the wind kicked up a little more. He knew he shouldn't stay there much longer, but the peace of the place—of the moment—was hard to abandon.

The clatter of hooves on the hard-packed ground broke the peace minutes later. He knew Meg had followed before he even looked her way. Pretty as she was, the woman was a bulldog!

She dismounted and ground tied Glory, then stomped right up to him. She'd changed clothes. Now she wore a quilted jacket and jeans that she'd tucked into her riding boots. Planting her hands on her hips, she just glared at him, her chest heaving as much as Apple Boy's had been.

''Generally a man gets to have a little peace out here,'' Evan charged, trying to look unaffected by her sudden appearance. But then again, what frame of mind did she expect to find him in after the way he'd ridden away? He uncrossed his ankles and stood, trying to make her back up a step. She held her ground even though it forced her to look up at him, her neck at an angle that exposed her long graceful throat. He took another step. Still she didn't give an inch, keeping that pugnacious expression on her face. Fine, maybe a rip-roaring fight would keep her at bay. "But then again a lady would generally know to leave a man alone when he seeks his own company."

She pursed her lips at that and turned away. He thought he'd won but she stopped after half a dozen steps, crossed her arms and whirled back to him, her blue eyes twin flames of fury. "My father said no one who did what I did for a living could ever be considered a lady again. I had to battle everything from poverty to lechers to get where I did, but I got there. I won. I *like* to win. If that makes me other than a lady, so be it. I don't care what you or anyone thinks of me. Not when I see you hurting Jack again. I made you his father by virtue of the adoption and if I have anything to say about it, you're going to be there for him this time."

Evan felt as if his head were going to explode. It had been too quick a transition from serenity to turmoil. He just couldn't seem to juggle it. His legendary calm deserted him. "You *don't* have anything to say about it," he yelled. "Frankly, neither do I. I *can't* go there! If I do she'll die. Don't you see that?"

She looked at him as if he'd come unhinged. Well, maybe it did sound that way. But a man had his pride, and he didn't need a woman he was attracted to standing there looking at him as if he was crazy. "Look, lady, just leave me alone!" he shouted.

"I thought I wasn't a *lady*," she said, clearly trying to egg him on.

It worked. He yanked off his hat and slammed it down on the rock. "You stand there all superior. Let me tell you something. You think you had it tough finding out Wade Jackson had been killed. Well, you don't know tough. You didn't watch him slip away an inch at a time. You didn't watch the confusion on Jackson's face when his mother couldn't lift him anymore. Or the anguish on hers when she couldn't find the strength to hold Cris's bottle. You didn't have to try getting her to eat, even though you knew that because of the radiation it would come back up anyway. You didn't have to hold her hand when some doctor said there was no hope—that she'd never see her baby girl take her first step. Never see Jackson go to his first day of school."

He raked his fingers through his hair. "Wade Jackson kissed you goodbye at an airport healthy and strong. Martha died in my arms, and it took six long months for it to finally happen!

"You think I can watch Jackson go through that all over again? He saw it all. Now I'm seeing it from his side. Jackson understands why I'm not there."

Chapter Eleven

Meg was spellbound by Evan's pain. He clearly did care about Jack and Beth. She had never stopped to consider any meaning for his absence other than apathy. But she'd been wrong.

"Jack may say he understands your not going to the hospital. And Beth's spent her life being ignored by her own parents. I'm sure she hasn't even thought of your absence as being odd. But it is odd. Very odd. I'm sorry this all brings back bad memories, but Evan, thinking history's somehow repeating itself is a foolish concept."

"Tell me that after Beth's gone," he snapped.

"Evan Alton, now is not the time to wallow in the pain of the past. The past isn't relevant right now."

Evan sank back onto the rock she'd found him sitting on and shook his head. She said a quick prayer that the right words would come to her. Otherwise Evan's relationship with Jackson might not survive.

"Your son—our son—is falling apart in spite of his faith. In spite of the fact that he's one of the strongest men I've ever met. In spite of visits from his pastor and Crystal and Cole. All my attempts to bolster his confidence are failing, even though he's trying to hide it. He needs you. Not messages. Not phone calls. *You!* Now what are you going to do about it?"

Evan said nothing. How was she supposed to reach him? His unreasonable fear—and yes, he was afraid—was as impenetrable as a foot-thick wall.

Help me do this, Lord. Just help me do the right thing where he's concerned. Help me touch him but not be touched by him.

She blinked. Prayer. What was the matter with her? Prayer was her answer! She walked back to Evan where he sat with one foot on the rock, his arm resting on his bent knee, his expression distant as he stared out over the barren plain.

Meg lowered herself onto the big flat-topped rock close to him. Close enough that she could reach for his hand. Somehow Meg managed to ignore the quickened pulse his nearness and touch caused.

Evan didn't react except to stare at their joined hands. Meg would forever be thankful she didn't have to look into those enigmatic stormy-sky eyes of his.

"Lord, God," she prayed aloud. "I ask You to reach down Your healing hand and touch Evan's heart. Give him the courage to go to the hospital. To minister to our son. To offer the comfort Jack so desperately needs from him right now. Show Evan how to be the father both Jack and Beth need him to be just now. Take away this irrational fear the enemy has placed in his heart to stifle his relationship with our son. Go with him into the lion's den and shelter him as You did Daniel. Be with him when the fiery furnace of his fears seems to wrap around him, just as You did with Daniel's three friends. Show him that You will bring us all safely through this trial. In the name of Your blessed Son we pray."

She sat utterly calm now, Evan's hand in hers. But then he looked up and captured her gaze with his. Her heart, which had settled down, took off on an unruly canter.

"Jack's lucky to have you in his corner, Meg."

"And I'm lucky he found me. But it's you our son needs."

Evan started, surprise in his gaze. "You said that before. *Our son.* I wasn't sure you saw me as his father. Not his real father. Since he found you I've felt sort of like a second stringer."

"Well, you aren't. If I've contributed to that feeling, I'm sorry. Of course you're his father. Wade isn't here. He was never here. You were. For both of us. When I needed someone I could trust, you took him and kept him safe. Now Jack needs you more than ever.''

Miraculously, he nodded. She could read his eyes now. He was going, but had no clue where the strength would come from. ''You coming, too?'' he asked, his voice husky.

''If you'd like,'' she promised.

Evan sighed. ''Yeah. If I start to fall apart—''

''You won't,'' she cut in, squeezing his hand. ''Just lean on the Lord. He's a lot stronger than I am. He can do anything but only if you let Him. The wife of our pastor back home once told Beth the Lord doesn't give us a spirit of fear. That fear comes from Satan, who uses it to take our eyes off God's grace.''

Evan nodded. ''I think she's right. I think every mistake I made with the kids was because I was afraid to let them get too close, for my sake and theirs. I convinced myself it was better not to love anyone too deeply, because they could leave me unexpectedly. I forgot how much being lonely hurts.'' He graced her with a sad smile and squeezed her hand. ''Let's go see Jackson and Beth.''

They spent the drive into Greeley in silence, but for Evan it appeared to be an easy sort of quiet. His driving gave him time to think.

And Meg? Well, she needed the time for prayer. They'd connected on a level she didn't know how to handle. Now she was the one unsettled. Afraid.

Not of a simple trip to see Beth and Jack. She was alarmed that Evan had begun to call to her in more ways than she dared to count. And that just couldn't be good.

They found Jack in Beth's room. He sat in a chair next to her, holding her hand and talking in a hushed tone. But her eyes were closed—still. Her usually silky blond hair had lost its natural luster and body and lay limply on her pillow. Her creamy complexion was pale and alarmingly sallow. Jack looked up, crushed tears glittering in his eyes.

"Jackson," Evan said.

Jack stood, surprise and gratitude in his expression. "Dad?"

"Is Beth asleep?" Evan asked, approaching the bed, his pace hesitant but determined.

Jackson nodded. "I'm so sorry, Dad."

"What, that I came to see her and she's sleeping? Don't be silly, kiddo. Sleep heals. We'll hang around all day if we have to. Won't we, Meg?"

"Certainly," she promised.

"No. Not that she's asleep. That I didn't understand what this was like for you. When they brought the twins, I realized that I hadn't thought of them in days, except to point out the posters of them for Beth. It's like the whole world has shrunk to this one room."

Evan put his hand on Jack's shoulder. "Pretty soon Beth's going to rally and the world will still be there.

For now you're doing what you're supposed to be doing.''

"And if she doesn't?" Jack whispered, almost as if afraid to say the words.

Evan hugged Jack to him and clapped him on the back. "Then you'll go on. And I'll be here to kick you in the pants to make sure you don't do to Maggie and Wade what I stupidly did to you and Cris." He stepped back and grasped Jack by his shoulders, looking him square in the eye. "But she *will* rally. Now tell your mother and me what's happening."

They sat in the chairs, Jack on the edge of the bed. Beth slept on.

"I guess in a way there's good news," Jack began. "Some big shot from the CDC flew in last night. He ordered a new battery of tests this morning. He seems to feel the answer is at the hospital where the twins were born. He agrees that she picked up something when they did the Caesarean. He's there now. He promised us he'd figure out how to treat her if it takes him a week of all-nighters. Those tests really wiped her out, though."

He raked his hand through his hair, reminding her of Evan. Actually, now that she thought about it, many of Jack's gestures were Evan's. She wondered if either of them had ever noticed and wished she had a window to the past—a small Jack following his father, imitating the big man he wanted to be when he grew up.

"What kind of tests, son?" Evan asked, calling her out of wistful thoughts. She'd missed a lot, but she was here now when he needed her most.

Jack shook his head helplessly. "CAT scans, blood tests. If they keep this up, she'll need a transfusion."

Meg chuckled and patted his back. "It just seems that way, dear. It'll be fine now. Who called in this new man?"

"Actually, Doc Reynolds. He stopped in yesterday, and when he saw that Beth wasn't doing any better he called his friend from med school. He's a director with the CDC."

"Now we'll get some action," Evan said.

Jack got to his feet and headed to the window, staring out. Meg knew it wasn't the awful view that drew him. Roofs and brick walls must have been a trial to her son with his love for wide-open spaces. After a few minutes Evan looked at her and shrugged helplessly. He mouthed, "What now?"

She pressed her hands together signaling prayer. Evan rolled his eyes and smacked his forehead.

"Jackson, come over here," Evan said as he rose. "Let's pray together."

Jack sighed. "Honestly, Dad, I'm about all prayed out."

"Good thing I'm not. Come on, son. You have to hold on to your faith. At times like this, it's all we've got."

Jack walked to the bed and Meg stood to take his

hand. With his other he grasped Evan's and dropped his chin to his chest. It looked more like acquiescence to Evan's wishes than respect for the Lord. She looked around Jack to see if Evan had noticed. He had. Frowning, he studied their son. She could almost see his mind searching for a solution to Jack's uncharacteristic crisis of faith.

"Lord, I'm pretty rusty at praying out loud, but here goes. First, You know our hearts and how much we all love this young woman who came into Jackson's life and fulfilled his fondest wishes. You've doubly blessed us with Wade and Maggie and we humbly thank You. But those little ones need their mama. Jackson needs his wife. The sun would still shine without her, but it wouldn't shine as brightly.

"I stand here looking at my son in pain and my new daughter fighting for her life. I have money to burn and can't do a thing to help her. I think I know how Jairus in the gospel of Matthew felt when he approached Your Son to beg healing for his daughter. As it turned out she had already passed from this life, but You honored his faith in You by giving his daughter back to him. We beg You to honor our faith and prayers in the same way. Please heal Beth. Please guide the mind of this new doctor. We believe nothing is beyond Your mighty touch.

"We believe You can heal our Beth. But we don't know Your will and that makes us all afraid of what the future holds. It isn't a lack of faith but our small, shortsighted minds at work here. Please give us peace. And again, please give our Beth back to us.''

And Beth's hushed voice whispered, ''Amen'' with them.

Chapter Twelve

Two days after visiting Beth in the hospital, Evan woke to the ringing of the phone next to his bed. Instantly alert, he rolled over, hitched up on his elbow and snatched it up. "Yeah?"

Jackson chuckled at the other end of the phone. "I actually woke you?"

Evan glanced at the clock on his bedside stand. He stared at it in disbelief. This is what came of thinking too long into the night, he mused. He hadn't slept until eleven o'clock in years. In fact, he didn't know if he'd ever slept this late. Surprise gave way to comprehension. Jackson had laughed. Evan smiled, rolled to his back and sank onto his pillow. "I'm assuming you have a good reason for interrupting my beauty sleep," he said.

"Beauty sleep? Right. Beth's much better, Dad.

She has a lot of strength to regain, but they say she's turned the corner.''

Evan realized once again that he'd lost a lot of his anxiety over Beth's illness two days before. Meg's prayer as they sat by Half-Pint Spring, and his own later in Beth's hospital room, had bolstered his faith and his hope. He'd begun to believe Beth would be fine, exactly as he'd been pretending with Jackson all along. "I'm so glad, son. I guess your mother's just as thrilled.''

"Actually, I called you right after I called Adam at the hotel. Would you pass the word? I'm going over to the room to catch a few hours' sleep. Last night it was a waste for me to try to sleep, so I sent Adam and Xandra back to the hotel and sat up with Beth instead. They're on the way here to spell me.''

"Well, I'm relieved to hear you're going to get some shut-eye. Exactly how is Beth doing? I'd like to be able to tell everyone here.''

"She's sleeping peacefully, with only a low-grade fever. She had a little to eat and she talked to me for about ten minutes. Adam and Xandra really don't need to come over, but they insisted.''

"You know you'll sleep better knowing someone's with her. Call later, okay?''

"Will do, Dad. Don't forget the folks at Laurel Glen.''

"I'll have Meg call them.''

They said goodbye and Evan jumped up. After

dressing quickly, he hotfooted it up to the main house. "Meg!" he shouted. "Meg, where are you?"

She walked to the railing, peering over as he ran up the stairs. "Goodness, Evan. Where's the fire?"

"No fire," he called as gained the top of the steps and swung around to face her. His heart felt light as air. "It's a celebration," he said, and gripped her by her slender shoulders. "Jackson called. The Lord came through for us. Beth passed the crisis! She's going to be all right." Without much thought at all, he lowered his head, pulled her closer and dropped a kiss on her lips.

And his heart felt as if it might explode.

He supposed he could blame it on celebration. Or triumph, even. But after taking a rapid step back, he realized that while it was all those things, it was more. He stared into her eyes, speechless. She seemed equally dumbfounded, her laser-blue eyes wide with shock. But he wasn't about to press her. Not until he understood the implications himself.

"You…uh…you call Laurel Glen, okay? I—I overslept. Are Cris and Jim riding, the way they'd planned?"

Meg nodded—her cheeks pink, her voice still obviously not functioning.

"I'll just go find them," he said, and backed away. Finally able to drag his eyes from hers, he turned and fled.

Heart racing, he headed for the barn. He didn't

really want to find Cris and Jim at that point. Shaken by the rush of feeling and physical response he'd thought had died with his wife, he couldn't deal with anyone at the moment.

He stopped and leaned his back against an upright post of the corral for support. His legs were actually shaking. The muscles felt as if they'd turned into jelly. He would mount Apple Boy and go for another hard ride, but he wasn't sure his quaking muscles would cooperate.

He narrowed his eyes, thinking back. He didn't remember even Martha inspiring the sort of explosive sensations that kissing Meg had caused. It had been years, but he knew his yearning for Martha hadn't been this fierce. It had been sweet and gentle. Like Martha herself.

"What's happening to me?" he asked the sky. "I'm supposed to be past being ruled by hormones."

For perhaps two minutes Evan actually relaxed. Hormones were a completely physical response. Meg had been affecting him physically since practically the day she'd arrived. This was just more of the same thing, then. And now that he knew what was happening, he'd just fight it more conscientiously. Mind over body. He wouldn't be ruled by animal instincts.

Then he remembered why he hadn't been able to sleep the night before. His thoughts had centered on Meg. And those thoughts had had nothing to do with physical responses. He'd remembered the day he'd opened up to her, and he'd recalled with perfect clarity the way she'd immediately clued in to the source of his most profound hurt. He'd remembered her strong faith and the way it touched and inspired those around her—himself included. Because of her influence, his faith had grown by leaps and bounds in the past week. How did a man fight that sort of emotional and spiritual appeal? Especially when there was such a strong physical one, too.

"You look like a man with something on his mind," Jim said from the middle of the corral. Evan turned, surprised he hadn't heard Jim ride in. As his son-in-law dismounted, he handed Duke's reins to Tomas—someone else Evan hadn't noticed.

Hoping to avoid Jim's uncanny ability to read people, Evan called to Tomas, "How's Anna today?"

"She is much better. If you need her, she can start working a little again soon."

Evan shook his head. "Cris and Jim should be here till Sunday, and Beth's brother and wife may be on board up at the house for the rest of the week, too. You tell Anna I said to take it easy and get stronger. We don't want her pushing herself. We'll need her soon enough. Beth's going to be coming home before we know it."

A man of few words, Tomas nodded and led Duke toward the barn.

"Okay, so we aren't talking about you today," Jim

quipped. "When did Adam and Xandra decide to come here?"

"It's really just an assumption on my part. I don't think anyone's going to need to stay with Beth when Jackson can't be there. He called. Beth's turned the corner according to her doctors. Where's Cris? I was actually looking for both of you so I could tell you the good news."

"We ran into your foreman. She went with him and I headed back before I overdid it and couldn't walk tomorrow."

"You still working on that novel in your spare time?"

Jim nodded. "Crystal read my second draft. She says it's good. She suggested changes to the ranch lingo, which I'll make, and then we'll see if it goes anywhere."

"Well, good luck. So where were Cris and Seth headed? I may ride out to join them."

"They said something about checking a fence line to the northwest. So, you want to talk about it?"

"Talk about the northwestern fence line?" Evan said, pretending innocence.

"Aw, come on, Evan," Jim ordered as he leaned on the fence from the other side. "Knock it off. I know you're having trouble with your feelings for Meg Taggert."

A horrible thought occurred to him. "It's that obvious?"

Jim shook his head. "No. But I've been exactly where you are. Maybe if we talk about it you can avoid some of the problems I ran into."

"You wound up married to Cris. I'm not going there again."

Jim chuckled. "If you only knew how much you sound like I did. So what's wrong with Meg? All the right vibes are in evidence whenever you two are in a room together."

Vibes? There were vibes? He thought for a moment. Yeah. There were. Both the physical and emotional kind. And that was his problem. She was a triple threat because her appeal was on three levels. Physical, emotional and spiritual. He was afraid that was a pretty tough combination to fight. "I don't want to feel what she makes me feel," he admitted. "But I'll figure out how to resist it. I just need time."

"Maybe you don't have the time. Fight too long and you may be too late for a good thing. What you need is to quit fighting your feelings and just go with them. I ought to know."

Jim sent Evan a look that spoke volumes, then turned and sauntered away. His son-in-law had once lost a fiancée to a violent death and had denied his feelings for Cris for so long he nearly lost his chance for happiness with her. But Evan didn't love Meg. He was attracted to her. Respected her. He'd even go as far as saying he enjoyed spending time with her.

He winced, remembering a talk he'd had with Jim

when he'd at last surrendered to his feelings. Evan did indeed sound just the way Jim had then. Did that mean it was already too late? Was he already in love with Meg Taggert? And if he was, did he want to do anything about it?

He didn't know. Which, in its way, was an answer. This would all require careful consideration. Meg was in his life to stay by virtue of her relationship to his son so there could be no false moves. Any mistake would cause embarrassment to himself and Meg that would last for years to come. Until he knew what he wanted to do and how he wanted to move forward, he had to guard his growing feelings.

Evan pursed his lips. It seemed as if he had some decisions to make. But that might not be the first task. Maybe he needed to know how Meg felt about him. And what she'd felt when their lips met.

Of course, he couldn't just ask her. He'd have to gauge her feelings by her reaction to him when he saw her again, but whatever her answers were, caution would have to be his watchword.

Meg sat in her room. Dazed. It was as if her brain refused to function. Evan had kissed her.

And she was in big trouble.

Because it hadn't been a romantic kiss. At least, not on his part. But to her…well…fireworks had seemed to burst inside her. Things like that didn't happen every day. Not to her, anyway!

She'd felt almost like the heroine in one of the romantic comedies she'd used to act in. And what was worse, she was very afraid her eager response to his lips had given her away.

The poor man had been overcome with delight over Beth's recovery. He'd kissed a friend in his exuberance. And she'd felt something she hadn't felt in years—if she had ever felt like that. It was as if she'd had no control over her feelings!

She wrung her hands. He'd been repulsed by her forwardness. That must have been it. He'd looked so shocked. Then he'd practically recoiled. Practically shoved her away.

What was she to do now? She couldn't leave. She'd promised Jack and Beth she'd stay for a while. Perhaps if she acted as if nothing had happened, he'd think he'd imagined her unruly response. He'd blame himself.

That was it! She'd pretend nothing had happened except a standard friendly kiss. She'd been an actress. Now was the time to pull out the talent God had given her and use it. She'd fix this by acting unaffected. Above such wayward thoughts. Now, if she could only make herself believe it, all would be well.

After calling Laurel Glen, she checked on the babies, first carefully sneaking a peek to make sure Evan wasn't with them. The coast was clear and the twins were sleeping peacefully. She found Jim in the living room, one of the baby monitors sitting next to his cup of coffee. He told her Crystal would be back from a ride soon and that he was on duty.

A ride sounded like a wonderful idea. Meg needed to clear her head. The Circle A was huge—easily five times as big as Laurel Glen—so she should be able to find a way to spend a few hours alone.

She noticed it had grown a bit colder, so she went back for a warmer jacket, the smart little ski hat she'd picked up in the hospital's gift shop and a pair of riding gloves.

There was no one around when she reached the barn, so she saddled Glory herself and led her out of the building. She'd just mounted the big gray horse when she heard Tomas call to her. "Where are you going? Señor Evan say it will snow," he told her in his slightly halting English.

"Oh?" She looked at the bright blue sky. It didn't look like snow to her, but she'd always loved riding with snowflakes falling gently about her dusting the ground and clinging to the trees. "That sounds perfect! Freshly fallen snow is always so pretty. At any rate, I probably won't be gone all that long."

"But it is so cold!" he protested.

Was it? She hadn't noticed. Maybe she was just made of sterner stuff. Winter in Pennsylvania had the kind of dampness that simply chilled to the bone. This was nothing. She smiled. "Don't be silly. It feels invigorating, Tomas. Don't worry about me. I was practically born in the saddle,'' she called over her shoulder.

''No. No. You do not…'' He was still protesting as she rode away. Checking the position of the sun, she rode due east, deciding to explore a part of the ranch she hadn't seen. An hour later the sunshine dimmed abruptly, drawing her attention upward and behind her.

''Oh, my goodness. That sky certainly does look like snow now,'' she told Glory. ''I guess we should head back.''

Meg wheeled the Irish Draught around and headed back the way she'd come. The wind kicked up, blowing fiercely and dropping the temperature within minutes. She pulled up her collar and buttoned her coat to the throat. Under her Glory grew nervous. Then Meg grew anxious, too, as the clouds thickened and obliterated the sun she'd been using to navigate.

Almost as if nature itself were conspiring against her, snow began to fall. But it wasn't the kind of snow she was used to. No gentle flakes, these. She'd never seen anything like it off the stage. The snow came down heavily as if being dumped in front of wind fans by the boxful. But this was no theater prop—these flakes were cold and wet. Meg pulled Glory to a stop and peered around. Nothing looked familiar. She didn't know if she'd lost her way or if the scenery just looked different with a white coating and no sunshine.

Then she remembered Glory. Horscs usually return to their barn on instinct. "Do you know where we are, girl? Suppose you get this stubborn woman out of a jam." Slackening up on the reins, Meg gave Glory a little encouragement with her heels and the horse leaped forward, then veered off to the right, an entirely different angle from the one she'd had them heading in.

This wasn't good. How off course had she gotten?

Chapter Thirteen

Evan knew he should probably leave buttoning the place up to Seth Stewart, so he tried to get his mind off the ranching operation. Instead, he checked both the house and the cabin and called Anna to make sure she and Tomas had everything they needed at their little house in case the snow turned into a full-fledged blizzard. The start of the snowfall had brought him to the realization that he'd spent too many years building the Circle A into what it was, to be able to just step aside while Jackson was away. But he didn't want to look as if he were circumventing his son's orders, just in case Jackson had been in touch with Seth. So Evan wandered down to the barn.

Everything looked fine as he walked around the buildings and corrals. Then he strolled into the main barn and the conversation he found there stopped him in his tracks.

Seth stared down at old Tomas, a worried frown on his face. "Tomas, you should have said something before this," the foreman admonished the horse wrangler.

"But she say she will not be out long time. I thought she come back. Then the horse is still gone when I finished with the other jobs you say I should do. I tell her she should not go. She say snow is pretty."

"Well, doesn't this beat all? Stupid easterners!"

Now Evan's heart froze in his chest. He'd have sworn time actually stopped. "Mind telling me which stupid easterner you're talking about?" he asked, but he knew already. Xandra was still in Greeley. Cris certainly wasn't an easterner and would know better than to ride out into the teeth of a Colorado snowstorm.

"Your guest, Meg Taggert, Mr. Alton," Seth said. "Apparently she rode out over an hour ago. Tomas—"

"I heard what Tomas said. Meg's not stupid, Stewart," Evan snapped. "She just isn't used to our erratic weather. No one from Pennsylvania would think this could have blown up the way it did. Yesterday was picnic weather."

Evan grabbed his gear, unlatched Apple Boy's stall and started saddling his surefooted quarter horse. "I'll go after her. Get some of the other men mounted up. You better get on over to your place and batten down the hatches. Did you see which way she headed, Tomas?''

"East.''

Evan looked over the saddle at the old wrangler. "Please tell me she was at least dressed warm. Hat? Gloves? Heavy coat?''

Tomas nodded. Evan pulled the saddle's cinch tight around Apple Boy's girth and slid the halter back onto the horse's neck. He put his bridle on, then unbuckled the halter and tossed it to Tomas.

"Take a pickup home with you and watch for us, would you, Tomas? When you see us ride in, pull the truck into the corral outside the door. That way I can get her up to the house and warmed up and you can unsaddle and take care of the animals and put them up for the night.''

"I will be watching, Señor Evan. I am sorry. She promise she only go for small while.''

"It's okay. Seth,'' he said as he pulled a walkie-talkie off the shelf and unplugged it from its charger. "I'll head due east. Fan the men out on either side of me in case she's off course. Whoever finds her should alert the others. Let Cris know what's up, but tell her if Jackson calls, not to tell him about this. I don't want him trying to get back here in this weather. He's where he ought to be and he doesn't need a new worry.''

"Will do, Mr. Alton,'' Seth said. "I'm sorry this happened.''

He shook his head. "No more your fault than Tomas's. Don't give it another thought. If you knew Meg the way I do, you'd know she's probably calling herself worse than stupid right now. She's pretty headstrong, but I guess she's had to be."

And that's one of the problems with her life, he added silently as he mounted. He didn't think she ever let herself lean on anyone, count on anyone. In the midst of family she was effectively alone. Even with their son, she seemed to feel it was her job to comfort him, but Evan didn't think she would turn to Jackson if she needed him. Was that the legacy of Wade Jackson, because he'd left her alone and expecting his child?

Evan didn't think so.

He blamed her father. Meg's life choices and dreams had strayed outside the parameters the man had drawn up for his daughter and she'd found herself cut off from everyone she'd held dear. Her father might have been a Christian, but he'd been a worse father than Evan had been. And thirty years later the woman she'd become was still afraid to lean on anyone—trust anyone.

Evan rode east at a fast trot with the snow already accumulating in sizable amounts. He couldn't track her, so he did the only thing he could do. He covered ground quickly and he prayed. Or tried to. Unfortunately, fear seemed to have him by the throat and his conscience kept enumerating all the ways he'd been a fool about her.

First he'd alienated her right off the bat when they'd met. Then he'd continued taking his past out on her and assigning the worst possible motives to everything she said or did. She'd had to force him to see her for who she was. And after that, he'd still nearly failed their son by staying away from the hospital when Jackson needed him. Finally, when he'd had a chance to change and further their relationship, he'd retreated like a coward. He should have kissed her again right there on the balcony. It should have been a long slow kiss that would have told her exactly how he felt about her.

And that brought up another question. Exactly how *did* he feel about her? Deep in thought, Evan rode on contemplating the feelings that had been building in him since that day. It felt good to finally acknowledge them but he really wished he'd come to this realization sooner.

Panic gripped him. What if something happened to her? Would his grief be less severe because he'd been unable to face the truth earlier? No.

And he'd learned his lesson.

When I find her and get her safely home, I'll tell her how I feel, Lord. I promise. She might not feel anything for me, and she might not want a future that includes the two of us as a couple, but I owe it to her and myself to find out if either is possible.

But first he had to find her. So with no choice but to continue on amidst the stinging snow and chilling wind, he slogged ahead. Evan rode by instinct alone, praying for guidance and putting his faith in the Lord that He would direct the search. When the wind kicked up a notch and the snow began to fall even harder, Evan laid his heels into the horse's sides and moved him into a faster gait.

Meg saw Evan burst out of the curtain of snow as if Apple Boy had taken wing. Her heart thundered in time to the big quarter horse's canter. He looked larger than life. An icon of the Old West in a shearling jacket, with a Stetson pulled down low over his eyes.

"Meg!" he shouted over the howling of the wind when he pulled his horse to a stop next to her. "Are you all right?"

Meg shivered—not because of the cold but because of the intense look in his eyes. She nodded. "Tomas said it might snow. I thought it would be nice to ride in it. I didn't expect anything like this."

"Always remember this is Colorado, not Pennsylvania. Our weather makes yours look predictable!" He pointed to her right. "There's a line shack due north of here. About a fifteen-minute ride. We can go there and wait it out. It's fully stocked. We'd be fine until this lets up. Or we can head on in. It's about half an hour. It's up to you. How cold are you?"

Spending time stranded in an isolated line shack with Evan Alton just wasn't an option. She wiggled her toes in her boots. She still had feeling. "I'm not that cold. Let's just go home. I don't want to cause Jack any more worry than he's had already. I don't want him finding out we're both missing."

He stared at her for a long moment, his expression grim and questioning at the same time. "I'm fine. Really," she assured him.

Evan shrugged. "Okay. They're your toes in jeopardy." He pulled his walkie-talkie out of his pocket and told the other man on the search that he'd found her. "Let's do it, then before this gets worse," he suggested as he tucked the radio back into his coat pocket. Then he guided Apple Boy into a turn and started back the way he'd come, after waiting for Meg to catch up.

She hadn't thought the weather *could* get worse, but within minutes it had begun snowing horizontally and the wind changed, buffeting them from the front. Evan pulled up immediately and reached for Glory's reins. "Transfer into my saddle," he told her. "I'll be able to shelter you from the wind."

Meg stared dumbly at him. Well, she guessed she had her answer about Evan's feelings for her if he could so coolly invite her to sit that close. She relaxed, but only for a moment, because she realized she had enough unruly feelings of her own to cause a problem. "I'm fine here," she lied.

He shook his head and pulled off the scarf he'd been about to tie over his face. "Then use this. You'll have frostbite by the time we get in out of this if you don't."

"What about you?" she asked, and the answer was in his expression. He'd give up his scarf for her and ride with the wind and snow lashing his face. "Oh, no, you don't. I'm the idiot who went riding in 'a little snow.' Hold on."

He grinned in triumph, and before she could think about all the implications of her decision, Meg pulled her foot out of her stirrups and kicked her leg over Glory's head. Evan took his foot out of his stirrup so she could step into it, then he grasped her arm to help her swing from her saddle into his. She threw her leg over Apple Boy's rump, and in seconds she'd landed behind Evan in the roomy Western saddle.

Even in the subfreezing temperatures and through layers of winter clothing she could feel his warmth only inches away. Meg hadn't realized she was so cold, and she longed to lean into him. Instead she held herself erect and stiff, uncomfortable being so close to him. Evan handed her Glory's reins next, wanting her to tie them to the saddle. Her fingers were stiff, but she managed.

Determined to get no closer to him than absolutely necessary, Meg kept her hands behind her back. She held tight to the cantle, trying to balance on the thick leather that formed the back of the saddle. But then

Evan suddenly kicked Apple Boy into a fast trot, and Meg slipped forward with a jolt. She gave up then, circling Evan's waist with her arms and settling into the saddle behind him. She rested her forehead in the center of his back and closed her eyes, inhaling his scent and his warmth.

Unbelievably, she fell asleep. But as she drifted off she wished he didn't make her feel so safe.

Chapter Fourteen

Evan let out a sigh when the lights of the compound came into view. He could have said his relief was due to the temperature, which had continued to fall, or the sky, which had dumped a good twelve inches already. Or even because he worried that Meg had been exposed to the elements for too long.

But what really had him swinging his leg over Apple Boy's head and stepping out of the saddle as they rode into the barn minutes later was a need to put a little distance between himself and Meg. Having her so close during the ride had been a little piece of heaven and hell rolled into the same experience. Add that to the two tons of worry and fear he'd felt when Tomas told him Meg was out riding and you had a man ready to leap out of his skin, not just his saddle.

Once on the ground he pivoted quickly and

smacked the quarter horse on his rump, sending Apple Boy, with Meg still on his back, deep into the barn. Meg's mount, still tied to Evan's saddle, obediently followed. Evan knew there'd be plenty of time later for soul-searching, but now he fought the wind to close the big double doors, shutting out the elements. Then he brushed off his shoulders, dumped the snow off the wide brim of his hat and dragged his gloves off with his teeth.

"I'll call the house and let them know we're back," he told Meg as he picked up the phone just inside the door. "She's here with me, Cris. Run a hot bath for her, will you? We'll be up there in a minute or two."

Evan watched Meg try without success to get her foot in the stirrup. He hung up the phone, rushed to her side and took her foot, placing it gently into the stirrup.

"I guess I'm about done in," she admitted. "I'm sorry to be such a bother. I don't think I've ever been this tired."

"You aren't a bother." He grinned up at her. "A greenhorn maybe, but never a bother. You too stiff to get down?"

"Me? Never," she boasted, and stood in the saddle. In a split second she'd flipped her leg over Apple Boy's back and had landed in front of him. But the grin slipped off her face when she kept going on her way to the floor.

"Whoa there," he said with a chuckle in his voice, moving fast to loop his arms around her waist and keep her upright.

Evan looked down at her. Her blue eyes reminded him of twin sapphires as she gazed up at him in the dimly lit barn. He grinned and knocked some of the snow out of her hair and off her shoulders before it could melt. She looked adorable in her snow-covered ski hat with her cheeks rosy from the wind and her nose rivaling old Rudolph's. Utterly desirable.

And really exhausted. Someone as petite as Meg wasn't in any shape to face what he had on the ride out to find her. He loved her. There was no other explanation for the gut-wrenching panic he'd felt when he'd learned she'd ridden out alone.

He wanted desperately to kiss her, so he did. Her lips were cool to the touch, but warmed quickly. He breathed in her scent. She smelled of fresh air, snow and a hint of springtime from her delicate perfume. It was the kiss he should have given her earlier.

He lifted his head, pleased by her spellbound look. "Why did you do that?" she whispered.

He grinned. "Because I could and because I wanted to." When she still looked confused, he added, "You figure it out, sweetheart."

He understood now that what he needed to do was woo her. She could find a new way of life there with him at the Circle A but he had to show her. He also needed a careful plan—not rash action.

"Thank you for coming after me," she said, her voice a bit raspy. "And please thank the others who were out in this looking for me, too. I'm so embarrassed. I'm not usually so foolish."

So she was just going to ignore what was happening between them. "Don't worry about it," he told her, determined not to let her try to fool herself as well as him. "Now let's get you up to the house."

"But the horses—"

He nodded to the short man entering the barn through the corral door. "Tomas will see to them."

"I left the pickup running, Señor Evan. Is she all warmed up?"

"Will be once I get her up to the house. Thanks, Tomas," he said, and scooped Meg up into his arms. "Hold the door for me, will ya?"

"Evan Alton! Put me down!"

"Nope. You'll just fall down again," Evan told her as he walked toward the door and the waiting pickup. It was a relatively short walk to the house, but he'd walked it in snow like this and it wasn't easy.

"Are you trying to humiliate me?"

"Nope. I'm trying to take care of you. 'Bout time someone did, don't you think?" he asked, and deposited her on the front seat of the warm pickup. He closed the door, pleased to see an astonished expression on her face.

"What did you mean by that?" she asked when he climbed behind the wheel.

Evan shrugged, pulled out of the corral and drove up to the house. He didn't answer until he was in the parking area near the house. "I've noticed you take care of everyone. Whenever I've heard of something going wrong at Laurel Glen, I hear about how you were there to ride to the emotional rescue. Who takes care of you, Meg? You endured your loss of Wade and then Jackson all those years ago and no one noticed, did they? I just thought you might like someone looking out for you for a change."

She nodded, still stunned, either by the foreign concept of someone watching out for her or by his analysis of her life. She didn't immediately protest, so maybe he'd come up with the right answers while riding out to find her. He might have hidden from life by becoming a loner, but she'd done the same thing by becoming all things to all people at Laurel Glen.

They all ran to her with their problems. Leaned on her for moral support. Needed her advice and guidance. But from what he'd heard from Jack and Beth, no one ever made sure Meg had all she needed from life. She apparently thought she had a good life, but from where Evan was standing, all she had was a share of everyone else's troubles and the frequent trips she took to get away from them.

Well, if he had anything to say about it, he'd be

that someone and life would be so good she wouldn't feel the need to travel just to find a little peace. She could put down roots here on the Circle A, where Jack and Beth would raise their children and Cris and Jim would visit with theirs.

It wasn't as if Colorado was devoid of culture or beauty, after all. Denver was a thriving city with a symphony, theater and museums. And she loved to ride. Where better than the Circle A for that? He'd even set up an equestrian course for her. It would all work out if Meg could get to the place he had.

If Meg could let go of the past.

Meg sank deeper into the steaming water. What a fiasco! She'd gone out for a ride to get away from Evan and had wound up sharing a saddle, his arms, a kiss and the front seat of a pickup. The saddle had been bad enough, but when he caught her during her plunge from the saddle to the ground, her heart had done some sort of bizarre gymnastic move inside her chest. She'd looked up in surprise when he'd pulled her into his arms, expecting to see annoyance.

That look in his eyes had been anything but annoyed. Then he'd kissed her. And it hadn't been a quick peck the way this morning's had been. This had been a slow, toe-curling kiss that was too long and too short at once. After that she'd have dared even the most sophisticated medical instrument to count the quickened beats of her heart.

She'd been wrong. Evan Alton was anything but indifferent to her. As inexperienced personally as she was with men, his reaction to her was now crystal clear.

She refused to even think about it. Or about how it had felt being swept up in his strong arms. Goodness!

She sank under the water. Maybe she could do as her onetime theater-in-the-round character had in *South Pacific*. Wash that man right out of her hair. She sat up abruptly. Nelly Forbush hadn't succeeded in getting rid of Emile de Becque. And that had been fiction! What made her think she could do it in real life?

How could one person make her feel so many distinctly different emotions at once? Protected, afraid, wary, curious, cherished and endangered—they'd all filled her till she thought she would burst. It confused her and made her doubt the way she defined herself.

And she didn't like it. Not one bit.

She'd come to Colorado to help Jack with his babies, not to have her world turned upside down by his father. She certainly hadn't come to have her life and her family's treatment of her questioned by the likes of Evan Alton.

"Oh," she groaned. "If only he weren't so handsome and so nice!"

If only she hadn't promised Jack she'd stay to help until Beth was on her feet. If only she could leave for home the minute Denver International had a flight out.

But she had promised to stay for a little while longer so she couldn't leave.

She stood, grabbed the towel next to the big garden tub and got out of the cooling bath. First a nap. Then safety in numbers. It would be just fine. She was made of stern stuff.

"What do you mean, Crystal and Jim took the twins to see Beth?" Meg demanded of Evan three hours later. She'd slept for two hours, then spent the next one trying to decide what to wear down to dinner. It had to be the right outfit. Sophisticated and expensive looking enough to put Evan off, yet not so fancy as to alert Crystal and Jim that this was different from any other meal they'd shared.

She'd settled on a blue cashmere sweater dress with a mock turtleneck. She'd topped it off with a gold chain necklace and gold button earrings.

"Jack called and said he'd caught Beth crying because she misses the babies. Cris and Jim agreed to take them to see her."

"But we're in the middle of a blizzard!"

Evan laughed. "Come here," he said, motioning to the French doors. He threw them open.

No cold blast of air invaded the room. The moonlight sparkled on the snow-covered pines that surrounded the stone patio and on the pasture beyond.

"And *that's* Colorado," he said with a laugh. "Blizzard conditions one hour and this the next. The roads are perfectly safe for a four-wheel-drive vehicle. The plows have been through already out on the main road and I plowed the main ranch road. We know how to handle this out here, Meg. Except on horseback when it's still coming down, twenty-four inches doesn't hardly slow us down."

"Well. No, I suppose it doesn't. I should see to dinner, I suppose." She backed away and tried not to run for the kitchen. Taking a deep breath once she got there, she almost screamed when Evan spoke from just behind her, his hands on her shoulders.

"I made dinner while you were napping. It's all set. Italian wedding soup, lasagna and a salad."

She looked over at the table set for two. Candles. Pretty dishes. Interesting handblown goblets.

Oh, dear. It all looked so...romantic. This wasn't good at all.

Chapter Fifteen

"This looks very festive," Meg managed to say, her heart thundering and Evan's breath stirring her hair against the back of her neck. She took a hurried step forward and thankfully he let go of her shoulders.

"You sit on down. I'll put it on the table."

She sank bonelessly into the chair. But then good sense reasserted itself. There was a way to fix this. While he was busy at the oven, she surreptitiously moved her place setting down the table by six inches, then slid down the bench till it was in front of her.

Evan carried the salad to the table, and though he didn't seem to notice her shift, he slid his place setting toward her, and when he sat his knee brushed hers. Meg nearly shrieked at that, dropping the knife she'd been toying with. It clunked onto the place mat and she shoved her hands under the table, clasping them together.

"So, are you feeling okay after that scare you had?" he asked.

She blinked. She had to get it together. He wasn't talking about anything but her fateful ride. "I'm fine, and really, I wasn't scared at all. I knew the horse would return to the barn."

Evan looked at her askance. "No, she wouldn't have. At the angle you were headed when I found you, you wouldn't have come to the ranch buildings. Glory hasn't been here all that long, and she'd never been that far afield. The snow probably had her as confused as it had you."

That gave Meg pause. "Then once again I thank you for coming to my rescue," she said as graciously as she could.

He grinned. "It was my pleasure, Meg." He dipped his head then and said, "Let's pray and get to this dinner."

She watched Evan as he offered a prayer of thanksgiving for the meal and the celebration of life that it was. He thanked God she'd been found safe and that she'd been brought into his life to remind him of the Lord he too often forgot. He also mentioned Beth and Jack and prayed that Beth would be home soon. Just after he ended with an *amen,* the phone rang.

He hopped up to answer it and Meg took advantage of his distraction to move her place setting yet another six inches farther along the table. Evan returned with the soup bowls and stopped short, a puzzled look on his face as he lowered her bowl to the place mat in front of her. But the confused look cleared and she assumed she'd successfully pulled off her little maneuver.

"So do you want your next course served at the other end of the table?" he asked. "At this rate you'll be on the porch for dessert."

A teasing light sparkled in his blue eyes. .They were blue tonight, reflecting the royal-blue shirt he wore. Meg felt her face heat. "I just thought with such a big table we should spread out a little."

His smile spread. "Oh. Good. For a minute there I thought you were afraid to be alone with me. But you wouldn't have any reason to feel that way, would you?"

"Certainly not," she asserted, then realized that she might have just backed herself into a corner. There was a calculating look mixed in with Evan's teasing expression. Almost as if he was pleased with himself and her answer—the answer he'd maneuvered her into giving.

"That's right—you just said you don't scare easily. Good. That was Jackson calling from Beth's room, by the way. The twins arrived safely. He'd like to talk to you after dinner."

"Then I'd better get to eating it, hadn't I?" she said, and devoted her attention to her meal. It was probably the best Italian food she'd ever eaten. Unfortunately, at that moment the soup tasted like dishwater and the pasta like sawdust. But she gamely choked it all down, determined to hide her nerves. How dare the man make her nervous?

"How about coffee and dessert in front of the fire?" Evan asked.

The living room was a huge spread-out affair. Oh, why had she thought of that particular noun just now? Nothing like that could ever happen to her again. She quelled the urge to leap to her feet. "What a good idea. How can I help?"

"By going in and relaxing. You're a bundle of nerves tonight. I don't think I've ever seen you like this. I told you Jim and Crystal got there with the babies just fine. They may even stay in Greeley tonight so Beth can have time with them in the morning. Nothing else is wrong, is it?"

Meg called on her acting ability. "What could be wrong?" she calmly asked, then turned and fled at a leisurely pace. It was a studied gait she achieved by picturing *War and Peace* balanced on her head.

She entered the living room and studied the area like a general planning a campaign.

She eyed the lone leather chair. That would be rather obvious and might give away her nerves. The sofa was out, of course. With the odd way Evan was acting, he might want to share it with her. The twin rockers close to the fire were a possibility, but they were near the raised hearth. Evan might opt to sit there. He'd be closer than if they shared the sofa. The hearth was out for the same reason. He could get too close.

Meg was horrified when Evan outflanked her, carrying a tray to the coffee table in front of the sofa. He sat and looked up at her expectantly. Was he taunting her? Daring her?

Worry over impressions flew right out those floor-to-ceiling French doors. She plunked herself down in the nice oversize leather chair, choosing defense over appearance. Snuggling into the corner, she crossed her legs, then her arms and smiled.

"So," he said, not showing any reaction at all to her seating choice, "where are you going after here?"

"I've thought about a cruise to Hawaii since I'm halfway to the West Coast, but it isn't written in stone. I've been on so many cruises, they've begun to bore me. I belong to a travel club and often pick up bargains at the last minute, so I might check those out."

"Jackson said you often take off at a moment's notice. Any particular reason you don't plan vacations ahead of time?"

"Oh, I do that as well, but I like to stay fluid. What about you?"

He frowned. "Before I came here I traveled enough to last a lifetime. Spur-of-the-moment to me meant I didn't know where my next meal would come from or when it'd be. Roots. That's what I care about. How about you? You seem to be a rolling stone.''

''Appearances can be deceiving. I still live where my roots are. Laurel Glen was one of the original Penn land grant properties. You don't get much deeper roots than that in the United States unless you have Native American blood.''

Evan stood and brought her a scrumptious-looking multilayered cake-and-mousse concoction on a plate and a cup of rich coffee. She took them from him and nearly swallowed her tongue when he perched on the sturdy rolled arm of the chair, a mug in hand. Her hands now full, she felt hemmed in.

''But Laurel Glen isn't yours,'' he said.

Why had she never noticed how mesmerizing his voice was? She stared up at him, struck dumb by the play of the firelight in his hair and eyes. ''Roots are about family, not real estate,'' she finally managed to say.

''The family is really your brother's family, though.''

''That's true, but I helped raise Hope and Cole. We're closer than your traditional aunt, niece and nephew.''

''But Jackson is your family, now that you've found each other. And Beth and the kids. Maybe you ought to consider moving here?'' His fingers played in her hair, sending a tingle down her spine. "Be a part of this family?"

"Evan," she protested. "What are you doing?"

He chuckled, and again a shiver ran down her spine. "You can't tell?"

Meg slid gracefully to her feet and put the coffee and cake on the coffee table before turning to face him. "I don't do things like this."

All innocence, his eyes widened. "Things like what?"

"I don't have affairs!"

"Well, I'm glad to hear it. Neither do I. Nor did I suggest one." His eyes smiled even though his mouth didn't. Somehow that was all the more maddening. He was teasing her. "That isn't what I want, and I think you know it," he finally said.

"I don't date, either." She tried again, fighting to maintain her temper.

"Again—good to know. Neither do I. At least, I didn't. But I want to now. I want you to give me a chance to convince you to stay here. Not for Jack and Beth or the kids. For us."

"There is no us."

He smiled. "There could be."

She wanted to say yes. Panicked, she said, "No. Absolutely not."

"Why not?" he demanded, but his tone was one of infinite patience. The kind one uses with a recalcitrant child. She was not a child!

"Because…just because. I don't have to give you a reason. I don't answer to you. I don't answer to anyone." That sounded more childish than anything that had come from the twins' little bow-shaped mouths thus far.

"I didn't ask to be your father, Meg. I have children. Why can't you relax and see where these feelings take us?"

"What feelings?" she asked, deciding to play dumb.

Within the next split second Meg learned something about Evan she hadn't known. He could move with the speed of a panther. In less time than it took her to uncross her arms and prop her hand on her hip Evan was up and cupping her face in the palm of his hand.

"These feelings. The ones we both feel when we touch, when one of us walks into a room the other's already in, when I do this," he finished, then bent his head to press a kiss to her lips as he threaded his fingers in her hair. Then he lifted his head and smiled gently. "Those feelings, blue eyes. We owe it to ourselves to find out where this could take us. I'll see you in the morning."

And then the rat, the louse, the sneak left through the side door before she could come up with a rebuttal.

The sky had lightened with dawn's sunshine before

she admitted the truth. Her only reason not to explore her feelings was fear, and that she just couldn't admit. At least, not to him.

Evan didn't sleep all night. He'd walked home feeling lighter than air. Then worry and finally fear had crept in. Stupid. Why hadn't he stuck to his plan? A nice dinner. Talk of the kids. Learn more about her life. Tell her more about him and the things Colorado had to offer. Simple.

But then he'd followed her into the kitchen and found her frozen in the doorway. He'd put his hands on her shoulders thinking to ease her into the room, and he'd been lost. She'd telegraphed her awareness of him and an endearing nervousness that had hit him hard. And he'd veered off course.

Her rapid response reminded him of a spitting kitten—adorable and dangerous, defenseless and captivating. And he hadn't been able to stop pushing her buttons all night.

Knowing she was attracted to him made him feel so alive. And so frustrated. He was terrified she'd throw away this chance in order to protect her so-called perfect life. A life that from where he stood wasn't all that perfect.

It was all right, he told himself. She'd promised Jackson she'd help take care of the babies, and she would. He'd have weeks to get her to see that God had sent them into each other's lives to be more to each other than Jackson's other parent and Wade and Maggie's other grandparent.

He had no intention of giving up on his plan, though he'd blown it last night. But for today, he'd leave her alone. Let her regain her equilibrium.

Seth had asked him to check on a couple of sick cows over at his place to see if he knew what was wrong with them. Seth kept his operation going on a wing and a prayer while working for the Circle A. Evan made sure he was out nearly all morning.

Meg's rental car was gone when he returned, but he thought little of it, assuming she'd gone to see Beth. He was partly right. The first sign that he'd made things worse than he thought was a call from Jackson. It was an abrupt wake-up call.

"What did you do to my mother?" Jackson demanded without preliminaries.

Guilt weighed on Evan's shoulders. Fear twisted his gut. "Do? I didn't do anything. Why?"

"Because she's gone."

Gone? "Gone where?"

"Home," Jackson said, accusation in his tone.

Evan almost said, "But this is home." He stopped himself just in time.

"Honestly, and I asked her to go easy on *you*," Jackson went on, disgust evident in his voice. "I guess I should have tried protecting her *from* you."

If only he'd stuck to the plan. It was enough to make a grown man cry. But that never solved anything. And sure as the sun would set, he didn't want to ask for advice about women from his son. Especially when the woman was his son's mother.

"You're upset, so I'll pretend you didn't say Meg needed protecting from me. No female has ever needed protection from me. I wouldn't even smack Cris's fingers when she was a baby to keep her out of things."

Jackson huffed out a breath. "I meant emotionally, and you know it."

Evan didn't know why, but he lost it. "I don't know anything anymore. Did she say it was my fault she left?"

"No. Not exactly," Jackson said a little too carefully, giving Evan an uneasy feeling. "She said maybe she's a rolling stone after all and that I should ask you what that meant."

Evan knew it was a message for him. He didn't think you were supposed to feel it when your heart cracked and broke in two. "She went out riding and got lost in the storm. I found her and brought her home. We had dinner. I can't help it if she got spooked and ran like a coward," he told Jackson, but he was talking to himself, as well. He'd followed his instincts and he'd been wrong. "I'm sorry she broke her promise to you and Beth in the process. She's an adult and this was her decision. She didn't offer any other excuse?"

"Some nonsense about Cole and CJ. I know something did happen between them, but then Cole left so suddenly Sunday, I thought he was going home to fix it.''

"He and your mother had a long talk Saturday night. I went to the kitchen to lend a hand on cleanup before going home and I heard CJ's name mentioned. I didn't want to intrude, so I left by the side door.''

"Then I would have thought it got handled already if Mom told him to go home. It just seems sort of suspicious that she'd fly home now that Beth's coming home. I'm sorry, Dad. I wanted you two to get along.''

Oh, we got along, all right, he thought. Maybe we got along too well. "As far as I know we got on just fine. But son, I've learned over the years that we don't always get what we want. We'll handle the kids and Beth just fine alone.''

"We don't have to do that. Adam and Xandra are staying and his son Mark's flying in with Joy when she comes to get Jim and Cris.''

"It'll be interesting to have a teenager around the place again. I'll show him the ropes of a ranch. It'll give me something useful to do.''

"You know it doesn't have to be a hands-off thing for you with the ranch, Dad.''

It was tempting. Now that this wasn't going to work out with Meg, he'd need something to do, something familiar to get his mind off her. "I got an idea today about getting into a speciality breeding program with a select herd of cattle. You're right about eating trends. Lean meat, that's the wave of the future. And maybe I can help Seth get a handle on that place of his while I'm at it.''

"I confess to being intrigued. Sorry I jumped to the wrong conclusion about Mom. We'll talk when I get home."

"Sure thing, son," Evan said, but felt uneasy again. Why had that felt like a threat?

Chapter Sixteen

Meg sat on her front porch looking out over the rolling hills of Laurel Glen. She'd bundled up against the dampness and had armed herself with a steaming cup of coffee. It was a perfect March morning. Punxsutawney Phil had been really annoying this year with his six-more-weeks-of-winter prediction, but it was clear that winter had finally given up its stranglehold on Pennsylvania.

The bare winter trees that bordered the pastures and shaded the buildings dotting the landscape had begun to thicken with new growth—a promise of spring. It was Saint Patrick's Day, and the fields had begun to green up just in time for the "wearing of the green" in southeastern Pennsylvania.

She'd arrived home in time to welcome another baby girl into the Taggert family. Amelia left for the hospital to deliver little Rose Taggert only hours after Meg's limo had arrived at the quaint little cottage she now occupied. Cole had mended fences with CJ and they were now happy again, living on an adjacent property passed down from his maternal grandparents.

She'd thrown herself into helping with both the new baby and CJ when Cole was busy with his veterinary practice, until both women were able to fend for themselves. Amelia was her old self again, but CJ still had the cast on, so Meg often ran by to help out a little. She also had her work with the historical society. She had the big spring benefit to help plan for the group. Her life was full and busy. Just the way she liked it.

So why was she dissatisfied for the first time since moving to Laurel Glen to help raise her niece and nephew? Why did nothing feel the same anymore?

Because Evan Alton put doubts in your head.

He'd cast suspicion on her family. Her wonderful, happy family who had been through so much pain and turmoil and was now doing so well. But now she felt as if she were on the outside looking in. And that was just plain ridiculous!

She was happy as a free agent.

No one demanded an accounting of her time. No one missed her if she wasn't home at a specific hour. And she let no one down if she took off for parts unknown on an adventure.

But did that mean that no one cared at all about her?

That's what Evan thought, but he was wrong.

He was wrong about roots, too. They were important but transportable. She thought of the expression "Home is where the heart is." Evan didn't understand that or her relationship with the rest of the Taggert clan. That was all there was to that claptrap he'd been spouting.

The phone rang and she picked it up from the chair next to her. It was her niece. "Hope, how is Faith? Still down with the sniffles?"

Hope chuckled. "Are you kidding? She was up at six-thirty, tearing around with enough energy to run her father into the ground. And has. She took pity on him and fell asleep on his chest a few minutes ago. He followed within seconds." She sighed. "Honestly, I don't know where the time goes. This last month with the new students getting settled in was so busy I've barely had a minute to call my own. Since right now there's peace, I wanted to touch base with you. We never get time to just sit down and talk anymore. Are you okay, Aunt Meg?"

Meg heard the concern in Hope's voice. Hers was not an idle question. "How sweet of you to worry. But it's unnecessary. I'm just fine. Why would you think otherwise?"

"Well, you came home so suddenly last month. Beth was still in the hospital."

"But on the mend."

"I thought you'd stay till she came home and was on her feet."

"Adam and Xandra Boyer were there to take care of the babies and Jack was with Beth all the time. And then there was that man I had to put up with."

"Man? Oh, Jack's father. He seemed so nice when he was here visiting Crystal and Jack. What was the problem?"

"Oh, you know how some people just rub each other the wrong way. That's us. Oil and water."

"Oh. Well, now, that's a disappointment."

"Why on earth would my problems with Jack's father be a disappointment?"

"Aunt Meg! Think how romantic that would have been. You two have so much in common, Jack among them. Suppose you two had hit it off and you'd found each other after all these years because Jack came looking for you. That would have been wonderful."

Meg felt her heartbeat speed up. It would, wouldn't it?

No, it wouldn't! She'd loved her father and he'd cast her out of his life. She'd loved Wade and he'd been mercilessly ripped from her by death. She couldn't risk giving anyone that kind of power over her. She'd never feel that kind of disillusionment again. Or that kind of pain. Never.

"Have you been tippling the cooking sherry, darling? It's a bit early in the day."

"Aunt Meg! I'm serious. He's absolutely yummy-looking, and you know it. What's the problem?"

"He annoys me," Meg drawled. "Have you ever known someone who's gone to a counselor and has become an authority on how everyone else should live their life? That's Evan Alton. I think my life is just perfect, contrary to his take on it. I just couldn't stay until Beth came home and have her saddled with the tension he'd created between us. Oh, dear. I really must run. Would you look at the time? I promised to get CJ's lunch today and I have errands to handle first. See you later, darling," she said, and hung up after Hope said goodbye.

"So much for my family not caring about me, Evan Alton!" she growled, and took a gulp of her coffee. She stood, telling herself the beverage had been too hot and that was the reason for the tears flooding her eyes.

Lunch with CJ quickly shaped up to be more of the same. They sat across from each other in the informal little breakfast room off Cole and CJ's kitchen. Meg poured the tea and set the pot onto the place mat in the center of the round table. "There now," she said to Cole's petite blond wife. "What do you plan for tomorrow after the cast comes off?" she asked.

CJ simply tilted her head a bit and blindsided her. "Meg, are you all right?"

Meg blinked. What on earth was going on? "Of course. Why would you ask?" She longed to know, but hoped she wouldn't dislike the answer.

CJ shrugged nonchalantly and poured dressing on her salad. "I don't know. I've noticed you looking sad and thoughtful a lot of the time lately."

"Oh, don't be silly," she said, tossing off CJ's concern with a dismissive hand gesture. "I've just been puzzling out the spring benefit for the historical society. We've had more response than usual and the facility is on the small side."

"Where is it going to be?"

"The Duportail House. It's a lovely place. Early eighteenth century. Lots of history. It was Lafayette's headquarters when the Continental army was at Valley Forge."

"Oh. I've been there. A friend of Cole's had his wedding reception there. Why don't you rent tents the way Ross does for the Valentine's Day party?" CJ suggested, an air of disbelief in her tone.

"Now, why didn't I think of that? There are even stone terraces like Laurel House's to set them up on." Meg grinned sheepishly. "I feel so silly. I've been ordering those tents for years."

"You know, you've been preoccupied ever since coming back from Colorado. Are you missing Jack and Beth that much?'' CJ asked, and took a bite of her salad.

Meg took a sip of her tea to ponder a good answer. No matter how she tried to change the subject it kept coming back to the same uncomfortable place. "I didn't really have much of a visit because Beth was so sick and Jack was with her at the hospital the entire time she was there.''

"Then go back now that Beth's on her feet.''

She shook her head. "Not for a while. My nerves couldn't take it just now.''

"What gives? Come on. Talk.'' CJ could be a terrible strong-arm for all her smallness of stature.

"Evan and I don't see eye to eye about some things. It makes for uncomfortable moments.''

"Evan Alton? Really, Aunt Meg, you've never let anyone dictate what you do—even passively.''

"Evan isn't a passive man, dear. And he isn't dictating anything to me. Leaving was my decision. It's *always* my decision,'' she told CJ, drawing a startled look. She wondered what she'd revealed unwittingly. Whoops! Time for another change of subject. "Now, tell me. Is my nephew behaving himself these days?''

Evan dismounted and led Apple Boy into the barn. It was snowing again. It was as if the Lord was determined to remind Evan of the day he'd ridden out in the storm to find Meg. And the evening that to him had held such a promise of happiness.

The really annoying thing was he couldn't remember a winter that had had so many snowfalls and so little resulting accumulation. It seemed as if every time he mounted up, the sky sent flakes drifting to earth unexpectedly. Hauntingly.

A month.

She'd been gone a month.

And he couldn't remember ever being so lonely.

He'd been careful how he was handling it, though. Even though he'd entered into a partnership with Seth Stewart to develop a range-tough but tender steer, he hadn't thrown himself into the project to the exclusion of all else.

Evan made sure to spend quality time with Jackson and his family. And he'd taken his son's spiritual advice and found a Christian counselor. He prayed a lot, but hadn't yet found any peace with what had happened between him and Meg.

His life was full and varied. He was doing all the right things. But he was miserable and he didn't have a clue what to do about it.

"Why don't you go after her, Dad?" Jackson said as if in answer to his silent question.

Evan hadn't even realized he'd halted his forward progress into the recesses of the barn. He turned to Jackson, who stood in an empty stall.

"Huh?" he asked, stalling—pretending not to have heard.

"I said, why don't you go after her?"

"Her?"

"Mom! The woman you're crazy about," Jackson clarified.

"Don't be ridiculous."

"Are you saying you have no feelings for her?"

"Don't be ridiculous," he said again. Jackson fell silent and Evan continued on to Apple Boy's stall, confident that he'd dodged the bullet.

"Are you denying that you fell in love with her?" Jackson asked casually a few minutes later.

"Don't be ridiculous," he repeated, knowing he sounded like a broken record. "Whatever gave you that idea?" he added, trying to recover lost ground.

Jackson snickered. "I'm not blind. And I talked to Crystal and Jim before they left. I hear dinner with you two was a study in furtive glances. If it helps, they thought she did as much looking as you did. And the more I think about the way she acted that day at the hospital before she left, the more I think she was running scared."

Evan scowled and flipped the stirrup up over the saddle so he could get at the cinch to loosen it. Okay, so maybe he *should* talk to Jackson about this. After all, his son was happily married to the woman of his dreams. What harm could it do?

"If this little talk is supposed to be uplifting, I've got to tell you, it's missing its mark. A man does not want to hear that the woman he wanted to spend the rest of his life with was afraid of him."

"But that's good. Don't you see? Beth was scared to death of me. She didn't show it at first. She came back at me like a spitting kitten."

Evan raised an eyebrow. That was how he'd thought of Meg. He tried Jackson's idea on for size while carrying his saddle out of the stall. He tossed the saddle over its rack and turned to his son. That *was* what he'd thought or he wouldn't have been as aggressive with her that last night she was there. He'd scared her right onto that plane!

And that was only part of the problem.

"They all take her for granted, run to her with their problems, then go back to their lives. Then she goes on one of her adventures to either get away from all the tension or because everything is suddenly fine and she no longer feels needed. I tried to tell her that having them in her life isn't the same as having her own family—that you and Beth and the kids *are* her real family—but she isn't interested in changing her life."

"I think you're being too extreme about Ross and the rest of them. I think they care deeply for her." Jackson grimaced. "But maybe they do take her a little for granted, too. It's like she lives in this little slot labeled 'Aunt Meg' and they don't see any other possibility for her. Neither does she. And you're right about me and Beth and the kids. We'd love to have her here. So why don't you go change her mind?"

"I just don't know, son. I really messed up the last time I tried. Why do you think she left?"

"Pray about it."

Evan sighed. "You think I haven't done that? God isn't talking. All He's doing is snowing on me and reminding me of the last night she was here. And that reminds me of how badly I blew it with her."

His son's blue eyes, so like his mother's, twinkled. "You're praying. But are you *listening?*" he asked, and sauntered away leaving Evan pondering his son's question.

Listening? Was God talking to him? It was a light-bulb moment. Were all these hit-and-miss snowfalls they'd been experiencing God's way of talking to him? Was He warning Evan that there was no forgetting Meg, so he'd better do something about it? He was still pondering the question when Beth knocked on his door later that evening.

"May I come in?" she asked when he opened the door.

Sometimes Beth could be so proper, even standing on the steps of a cabin wearing jeans and a sheepskin coat. He grinned. "Anytime. What can I do for my favorite daughter-in-law?" he asked, smiling broadly, glad to see her doing so well and looking so healthy.

"You can go follow your dream. You can challenge Meg to come back."

Evan pursed his lips, shaking his head. Not to refuse necessarily, but because he still thought it would be a fool's errand. He walked away, leaving Beth to follow, and all but threw his body into the chair by the fireplace. He looked into its bare cavity and thought of that night in the main house in front of the warm and cozy fire. His idle hearth felt like a symbol of his life since she'd left.

Cold. Dark. Empty.

"The truth is, sweetheart, I'm not enough for her. She'd rather have her life go on as it is. Living where she's a Taggert. At the beck and call of a bunch of people who see her as an accessory in their lives. They take her out. Use her. Admire her. Then they put her back on the shelf while they go off and *really* live. She just sits around and waits to be needed again. Oh, every once in a while she gets this spurt of independence and goes hying off somewhere, but then she just goes back and climbs up on that shelf again."

Beth had sat across from him and just stared at him with the oddest light in her eyes. "What?" he asked.

"I didn't see it before. You've really thought this out. I guess you two must have really gotten to know each other."

"We talked a lot."

"This is what Jack meant earlier tonight when he said he'd begun to wonder if his mother was any happier with her life than you were with yours. I think you're right on about Meg. She thinks she has a life, but what she has is a part of everyone else's. The only thing she does for herself is her work with the historical society, and that grew out of some old papers she found years ago about Laurel Glen. I know she likes to travel, though now I wonder about the reason she does it.

"But, Evan, you're off as far as the rest of the family goes. They do love her and I know Cole is always telling her to basically get a life. Ross, too. Last year Hope even tried to fix her up with a visiting instructor at the equestrian school Hope and her husband run. It was awful. Meg all but patted the little guy on the head." Beth grinned. "He might as well have been a lapdog. He was all wrong for her. You, on the other hand, are exactly perfect."

That had him taking notice. Beth probably knew Meg better than anyone. She was a woman. Women knew about these things. He sat up a little straighter. "You think so?"

Beth stood. "I'll go home and have Jack see about getting you on a flight. I wouldn't count on anything until after the weekend, though. Oh, and I'll call Crystal to tell her you're coming for a visit. And why?" She grinned. "So you can't back out once you get there." With that she turned and walked to the door before looking back. "And Evan. Don't come home without her."

Chapter Seventeen

Evan flipped on his turn signal and drove under the iron entrance archway to Laurel Glen. Beth and Jack had been married beneath a replica of the apparently famous arch at the church they'd both attended near here.

He looked ahead at several pastures lined with crisp white fencing that stood out in bold contrast to the rolling hills. Remembering Jim's one-word description of Pennsylvania, Evan realized more than ever how well it fit.

"Green," Jim had said of the place in summer, but even now, at the end of what reportedly had been a rough winter, the fields were already cast with subtle shades of green.

Laurel Glen was picture-perfect, with its crowning jewel, Laurel House, in the distance atop a far hill.

The farm operation with its brick-and-stone stables and barns sat nestled below along with two cottages.

Evan parked Jim's cherry-red classic Mustang in the circular drive and started up the stairs. Six steps connected each of the three terraces and were offset from each other as if to encourage guests to slow down and enjoy the view. Evan turned when he reached the top level and did just that. He could understand why Meg returned here time and again. The peace and majesty of the place just seemed to seep into him.

Shaking his head in surprise that anything could calm him just then, he turned and rang the doorbell. As he waited, he sent a prayer winging heavenward that his love would be enough to convince Meg to give all this up.

"I'll get it," Ross Taggert called out as he sailed down the wide circular staircase, a nineteen-month-old limpet, who seemed convinced he was her pony, attached to his back. He'd noticed Jim Lovell's Mustang climbing toward the house. Ross absently wondered what the state police detective, now family member, might want. There had been a time when he'd have been worried—now he was just curious. Ross pulled open the door and got the surprise of the year.

"Evan?" he said, shocked beyond words. "I saw the car and expected Jim. I didn't know you'd come east.'' He extended his hand in greeting and chuckled as one of the little arms wrapped around his neck was extended, too.

''Hi! I Laurel!'' She pointed toward the stairs behind them. ''Baby!''

Evan smiled and took Laurel's proffered hand between his index finger and thumb and shook it. ''I know. I met you when *you* were a baby. My, how you've grown, little one.''

Ross chuckled. ''She's quicker than we can keep up with, believe me. So, what brings you to my neck of the woods?''

Evan grinned. ''I'd rather not get into it on the front step.''

Ross rolled his eyes. ''My manners seem to have taken a hike. Come on in. How are Jack, Elizabeth and the twins doing?'' he asked as he led Evan into the parlor off the foyer. ''Sit. Make yourself comfortable. Can I get you anything?''

Evan shook his head. ''Nah. I'm fine. Cris and I just finished lunch. I'm staying there for now.''

''Great. Let me just get this one passed off to the cavalry in the kitchen and I'll be right back.''

Ross puzzled over Evan's sudden arrival all the way to and from the kitchen. He'd reached no conclusions when he got back. ''So Cole says Crystal's expecting. There's no problem there, I hope.''

''Oh, no. I'm here for me. And hopefully Meg.''

Now, there was an answer he hadn't seen coming. "Meg?"

"I'm in love with her," Evan said starkly.

Why was he so surprised? Ross wondered. Meg was gorgeous. She and Evan had quite a lot in common, he realized now that he thought about what he'd heard from Jack about his father. But why tell *him?* "That's…ah…nice. Does Meg know this, or am I the first one to hear?"

"I'm pretty sure she does. I'm also pretty sure that's what sent her running back here where she feels safe."

Ross frowned. "Why would she need to feel safe from you?"

"Because I threaten all of this," Evan said, gesturing to the house.

The man's manner was too calm for Ross to consider what he'd said as any kind of attempt at intimidation. "How do you threaten Laurel House?"

He shook his head. "No, not your house. Not your farm. I mean her life here at Laurel Glen with your family. If you want to call it a life."

Now, this was intriguing. Evan Alton saw what so few others did. Ross chose to overlook the "your family" part of his explanation. He would get to that in a minute. Right then he was interested in what Evan had to say about Meg and, old-fashioned as it sounded, what the man's intentions were toward his sister. "What is it you'd call it if not a life?"

Evan didn't answer right away, but clearly gave the question a long moment's thought. "Existence, I guess."

"I don't know if that's a fair assessment. Of Meg's life or our family. She has friends, my wife among them. I'll admit I often feel she gives more than she's willing to take, but that doesn't mean the rest of us don't try. For instance, I never expected her to move into that cottage. For years I've done all she'll let me to make up for my father cutting her out of the will." Ross shook his head. "You ever try to make her take something she says she doesn't want?"

Evan grimaced, then smiled sadly. "Besides me, you mean?"

It was Ross's turn to wince. "Sorry. The Taggerts can be a stubborn lot, but I see you've found that out."

"I've dealt with a Taggert for thirty years, Ross. I know about stubborn. Luckily I've not only had practice on Meg's son, but I'm every bit as tenacious. I'm not giving up. That's why I'm here."

"That's why you're at Laurel Glen. But why come to me?"

"Because I'm going to have to wear her down. And I can't do that if I never see her. I understand you had to let your foreman go. I imagine you and Cole are pretty busy right now."

Ross gritted his teeth. Every time he thought of that nitwit he'd hired to replace Jack he got angry all over again. "I'm not letting Cole do as much as I probably should. He's got an injured wife and a full veterinary practice besides the work he does with our horses."

"And you're also shy a trainer."

"Actually, Meg started filling in there and Hope's tried to give me an hour here and there, but she's as busy as I am."

Evan grinned. "Perfect. I wondered if we could work out a deal. The use of the foreman's cabin in exchange for taking some of the workload off you."

Ross chuckled. "Oh, this is going to be good. But if Meg smells a setup, she'll be on the next slow boat to China or the next plane to Colorado to visit Jack while you're gone! You'll be playing plane tag. I think we better tread carefully and move into this so she doesn't catch on. Amelia was just saying she wanted to have a little family dinner party to introduce baby Rose to everyone. If we enlarge the guest list a little we can include Crystal and Jim, which is a plausible reason for you to tag along with them, since you're in town. Here's what we're going to do."

Meg handed CJ a cup of tea and sat on the settee across from her and Cole. "So, darling, how much longer are you going to be off the job?" she asked, and watched Cole's reaction carefully. The poor boy was still privately beside himself with worry over

CJ's accident. He put up a brave front, but his wise-cracks still had a bit of an edge to them, exposing his unsettled heart.

"I—I...um...I don't know. I promised I'd take it easy as far as riding goes. I'll be able to work some of the young ones on the lunge line soon enough."

"Then I'll continue helping for a while longer." Meg glanced at Cole to see his reaction, but her nephew's gaze was now fixed on the foyer. Then he grinned and there was an expression in his eyes she'd come to know over the years. Part mischief and part glee. It usually signaled trouble for someone.

"Would you look at who just strolled in with Jim and Crystal," he said, grin widening.

"Who?" Meg asked.

"Evan," Cole said, smiling more broadly.

Meg rolled her eyes. "Very funny. Did you really expect me to fall for one of your terrible April Fools' jokes?"

Cole made a dramatic grab for his heart. "You wound me. And who says I was joking? Look."

She did and was instantly sorry she had. Evan stood with his daughter and her husband, looking boldly handsome in a gray suede jacket and black slacks. He laughed at something Ross said and shook hands with him. Then the four of them sauntered into the parlor, stopping to chat with Amelia and ogle baby Rose.

Meg looked away when Evan took the baby. The

man did love babies. She gritted her teeth against the pain and anger raging inside her. What was he doing here? Was she to have no peace from him or the memories?

Her mind was in a turmoil, and that whole last night played itself over again in painful clarity. She yearned to go to him. To feel his arms around her again.

To demand to know why he'd intruded on her world!

However much she wanted to do just that, Meg absolutely refused to move—or to stoop to his level. Then a snicker drew her attention back to Cole. She looked at him and that wiseacre smirk of his. "When you were fifteen I would have sent you to your room for that rude noise *and* for wearing that expression."

Unapologetically he asked, "Are you going to just sit there?"

She arched an eyebrow. "A lady does not approach a man. You, however, were just his guest and he went to a lot of trouble to see you got to your plane. Go thank the man again for his hospitality and his help."

"Yes, ma'am," Cole quipped and stood, then he bent over her and whispered, "Care to send your love, Aunty Meg?"

"Go on. Get, you scamp!"

"He is so good-looking," CJ said.

"Cole? Of course he is, darling. He's a Taggert.

It's in their genetic imprint. As are that smart mouth and seriously twisted sense of humor. Only the women are spared.''

''I mean Evan Alton, Meg, and you know it,'' CJ insisted. ''Are you sure he's too aggravating? He seemed so nice the couple of times I met him when he was here before.''

Meg carefully folded her hands in her lap, proud they didn't shake. ''Oh, believe me. I'm sure. Nice.'' She said it like a sneer. ''Pandas look *nice,* but then you notice their claws and teeth.''

CJ frowned. ''So you're saying he's not nice?''

''I'm saying he's an arrogant, know-it-all cross between a horse and a donkey.'' She stood and winked at CJ. ''You figure it out.''

She had no idea what she intended to do next but, as she turned she found her gaze helplessly captured by Evan's. He started across the room toward her, rooting her to the spot. Maybe she couldn't seem to get her feet to obey, but she had no intention of letting him know how much he unnerved her.

Smiling politely, Meg held out her hand, bracing herself as she did so. She wasn't disappointed. Her hand slid into his, and the slightly abrasive calluses on his palms raised gooseflesh on the rest of her. She refused to shiver.

''Evan, you're certainly far afield,'' she commented coolly.

He nodded, smiling. ''I had some unexpected business to attend to in the Northeast, so I decided to spend some time with Cris and Jim before the baby comes.''

The doorbell rang. Ah, she thought, saved by the bell. ''How nice,'' she said. ''Have a good visit. If you'll excuse me, a very special man just came in. I really must make him feel at home.'' She stepped away and walked into the foyer, where Ross was handing Xandra Boyer's coat to Sally, Laurel House's housekeeper. Adam stood behind her and his son, Mark, hung back, looking as if he'd rather be tortured than attend a dinner party.

Meg charged right up to the boy, who was six feet tall and thin as a rail. His face lit as soon as he saw her.

''Mark. Just the man I'd hoped to see here tonight. Have you grown since I last saw you?'' she demanded, tilting her head up at an exaggerated angle.

Mark's green eyes brightened. ''Aunt Meg! I brought Dragon's Keep with me, just like I promised last time I was here.''

''Your new medieval video game?'' Mark nodded. *Oh, bless you, boy.* ''Stupendous! Dinner is about to be served, so playing will have to wait, but that should give me time to pick your brain. You're my dinner partner.'' She hooked an arm around Mark's thin arm and steered him into the parlor. ''I want help getting to at least the second level before the night is out, so don't try to get away.''

She glanced back over her shoulder and sent a smirk Evan's way. Her triumph was short-lived, however, because he raised his glass to her in a silent salute. Or had he just picked up the gauntlet she hadn't meant to throw down?

Chapter Eighteen

Evan watched Meg across the table, hardly able to take his eyes off her. She looked absolutely breathtaking in a light green jacket and slacks that reminded him of the Orient.

It was clear to Evan that she'd latched on to young Mark as a dinner partner to spite him. He tried not to let it hurt, but it did. He had to believe that if he hadn't been there, Meg still would have ridden to the boy's rescue. Mark was out of place at the dinner party and Meg was the type of person who would notice.

She was good, kind and generous. And he loved her.

Seeing her again was everything he'd hoped it would be and everything he'd feared. His heart thundered even as it ached with worry. What if he failed? How would he go home—go on—without her?

Please, Lord. Show Meg she belongs in Colorado with me. Please, please, guide us all tonight and forgive the trap we're about to spring on her.

"So, CJ," Ross said. "How did the appointment go? Did the orthopedist say when you can come back to work?"

Cole cleared his throat. "Actually, Dad, that's something we needed to talk to you about. CJ isn't going to be able to come back completely for about a year."

"Was it a worse break than we all thought?" Meg asked, a worried frown creasing her usually smooth forehead.

Oddly, Cole grinned. "No, but there's something I didn't know about when she got hurt. We're having a baby in October."

Amelia and Meg jumped up and hugged CJ, then Cole, and all the men shook Cole's hand. When everyone settled back down, CJ spoke up. "I'm not sorry about the baby, of course, but Ross, I am sorry to leave you so shorthanded. The doctor thinks with the break and the fall it'd be better if I wait to do any jumping or intricate riding until after the baby's born."

"Don't give it another thought. Family always comes first. You both know that," Ross said.

As expected, Meg stepped gamely up to the plate. "Ross, I can fill in with the training more than I do now. I know I've mostly stayed out of the operational end of Laurel Glen in years past, but I'm really enjoying working with the young horses." She grinned at CJ. "Under CJ's tutelage, that is."

Ross beamed at her. "Meg, that'd be great. Now, if I could just find a foreman."

"When Cole was at the Circle A, he mentioned that the guy who replaced Jackson didn't work out," Evan said, taking his cue from Ross.

"CJ's accident was his fault. I let him go. He broke my cardinal rule. He knew I won't take problem animals and he was aware that the owners were having serious trouble with that colt. Then he not only took him on, but he didn't warn CJ before she worked him. When I think—" Ross cut off the thought and shook his head, glancing at Cole. "No sense going there." Then he narrowed his eyes as if deep in thought. "So Evan, how long did you say you'll be staying with Crystal and Jim?"

"Not as long as I'd like. Their place is on the small side, but it's on a nice-sized piece of land. Jim and I drew up some plans to enlarge the house before the baby arrives."

Jim jumped in, filling in the details of the addition, and Cris explained a few of her ideas for the nursery they planned.

Evan grinned inwardly as he listened with half an ear while marveling at the way the conversation unfolded all on its own. Not only would he be living across the drive from Meg, but she'd already given her word to fill in for CJ. So now he'd be working around Meg, as well. It was amazing how clearly you could sometimes see the Lord's hand on certain situations.

"Unfortunately, my brilliant idea just did me out of a room," Evan added when Jim wound down. "Their extra bedroom is about to become a wide hall to the addition." He turned to Jim. "The construction starts in less than a week—right, Jim?"

"Yeah. A bunch of the guys from the church are going to help me do it myself. A lot of us worked on the Tabernacle with Jim Dillon when we converted it from a barn to a church."

"Then I suppose you'll be going back to the Circle A," Meg said. Evan tried to ignore the hurt caused by the delight in her voice, but it was pretty hard.

"And I'm so disappointed." Cris pouted. Evan fought a grin. Cris had never pouted in her entire life.

"He won't be leaving if I have anything to say about it," Ross put in. "If a daughter wants her father nearby when she's expecting her first baby, he should be there. And I have the perfect solution. The foreman's cottage Jack lived in is sitting empty. Why don't you just stay there?"

Evan pretended to contemplate the offer. "I don't know, Ross. It's kind of you, but I'd hate to take advantage. Have you ever rented it?"

"Evan, no offense, but I don't want to complicate my taxes. If you feel you need to contribute something, suppose you lend a hand on some of the foreman's duties. You can imagine how swamped I am right now with both positions empty. And I don't know how long it's going to be before I find a new foreman. If you could handle work assignments and a few other jobs, it would help out tremendously.''

He carefully glanced at Meg. She looked shell-shocked, and Evan had to bite the insides of his cheeks to keep from grinning and giving them away. After a beat he said, ''You know, I could use a crash course in this kind of operation, considering the direction Jackson's taking the Circle A. You're on, Ross. I could use a challenge right now.''

And winning not only Meg's heart but her trust was the most important challenge he'd ever faced.

Sunday morning, three days after Evan's surprise appearance at dinner, Meg crawled sluggishly out of bed. If she didn't get an unbroken night's sleep soon, she'd lose what was left of her mind. It had been bad enough with memories of Evan haunting her dreams.

Now he'd be haunting her waking hours, too!

He'd be living across the drive from her, working around the farm, trying to wear down her resistance by fair means or foul. Oh, he hadn't fooled her. He hadn't had business in the area. He was there to convince her to go back with him. And it wouldn't work.

She didn't love him. Couldn't love him. Refused to love him.

Even if she did—and she wasn't admitting she did—she'd go mad buried in Colorado where his so-called roots held him prisoner in a stagnant life.

Meg splashed water on her face, dressed, then stumbled to the kitchen for some coffee to kick start her day. As she sat at her kitchen table staring into the dark cup of liquid, she admitted that lately some of her trips *had* lacked something. She had indeed taken a few of those trips to escape family stress. Still others she'd planned to avoid an empty feeling she often got when she was no longer needed after the resolution of a family problem. Evan had been right about that, too.

But just as many other trips in the past years had added richness and excitement to her life. And would to Evan's if he'd just give it a try. How could anyone look out over the Sea of Galilee, stand at Calvary or gaze at the empty garden tomb and remain the same person? How could someone not grow as a person after viewing the artistry of the Louvre and the Sistine Chapel, or feeling the pain and horror of Auschwitz? She would be a poorer person without her travels.

She had more places to see. Many more things she'd promised herself she'd do. Meg didn't want to give all that up to stay put forever in Colorado.

But what about Evan?

Meg bit her lip and pushed away from the table, blinking back sudden tears. One foot in front of the other, she told herself. Dress for church. Go for a ride. Shower and change for Sunday dinner at Laurel House. One more day behind her. She stopped halfway through the living room, staring out the picture window at the big chunky flakes drifting to the ground.

Snow flurries.

Again.

On April fourth! Winter refused to end. Would the snow never stay away?

Then, sliding across her mind as silent and stealthy as those soft flakes, the sight of Evan riding to her rescue assailed her. *There are sights and then there are sights,* a voice inside reminded her. *None of your travels ever gave you an experience like that one. That was really living!*

Caught up in the memory, she realized the whole day had started to play across her mind. Determinedly, Meg slammed her eyes shut, banishing the memories with a shout. "Okay!" she yelled to the empty cottage. To the taunting voice. "I love him. There, I said it!" She sank onto the sofa, tears flooding her eyes.

But how could she give up all she had for the uncertainty of a new love? At her age? Evan expected her to give up too much—Laurel Glen and all it had meant to her for so long. Risk too much—security, familiarity, the love of everyone in her life. For a way of life she wasn't sure she could bear.

For him.

She couldn't do it. She was just too afraid.

Jim Dillon, the pastor of the Tabernacle, strode from the back of the sanctuary to the stage and bounced up the steps as laughter continued to ripple through the congregation after a joke he'd cracked at the end of announcements.

"I know I said we'd finally finish up Psalm 119 today, but last night as I was praying the Lord put a couple of verses on my heart. Considering their content, I decided I should listen. They're short, sweet and to the point, so don't bother turning there. Proverbs 3, verse 5—'Trust in the Lord with all your heart, and lean not on your own understanding.' And verse 6—'In all your ways acknowledge Him, and He shall direct your paths.'

"This, my friends, isn't as easy as it sounds. Because sometimes the Lord expects us to follow Him down paths that look to our blinkered eyes like minefields. And we start doubting Him. He must get so sick of hearing, 'But, Lord' from all of us.

"We aren't alone in this failing. Many great men have cried out that same thing. Moses, Jonah, Gideon. They all said, 'But, Lord.' Sometimes, like Moses, we follow those two words with excuses for why we aren't up to the challenge the Lord has set before us. Or we ask, as Gideon did, for a sign that we're seeing the same road He is. The Lord, ever faithful, sends us the sign we need. Some of us see the sign He sends and finally act, but others still want another sign and then another.

"I've been working on listening to His direction for some time now. Those of you who were around in the beginning of the Tabernacle know how long I tried to pretend that I wasn't a pastor and that we weren't a church." He whistled and shook his head, an embarrassed grin tipping his generous mouth up at the corners and crinkling his eyes. "I'm surprised this isn't called Tabernacle Bible Study to this day."

Everyone laughed. That Jim Dillon hadn't counted himself worthy to serve the Lord was a well-known fact at the Tabernacle. That he served his Lord well and with humor was another.

"My point is that if the Lord has a road He wants you on, but you persist instead to travel the road you've chosen..." He sighed and shrugged. "Think of Jonah. Bet he wished he'd listened during that three-day ride to Nineveh in the belly of that fish. Ever been in a fish market at the end of a long, hot day? Phew! Not a pretty thought. And can you imagine how he felt when he looked around on that beach and found himself in Nineveh anyway?

"Another thing I've noticed about people who don't want to listen is that they always say, 'If God would just talk to me the way you are, I'd be sure it came from Him.' Uh...remember Moses? The burning bush? Didn't work that time, did it? I think God must have been really frustrated by that one.''

Meg thought about the snow earlier. Had that been the Lord's way of reminding her of Evan? And what about Evan needing somewhere to stay and ending up at Laurel Glen? Even if that had been some sort of setup, what about Ross being all but buried in work? And CJ needing to give up training because of the baby? None of that could have been arranged beforehand.

Even so. How could she put her trust in Evan?

''Now I want to back up to the first verse I read. We need to trust in the Lord that these paths He wants us to travel, however rocky, impossible and downright scary they look, are the paths He wants us on. The road less traveled is often His choice for us.''

Meg let Jim Dillon's voice fade away. She closed her eyes and prayed. *I promise to try, Lord. I promise to keep an open mind. But You'd better have a chat with Evan, because I can't give up my way of life, my family and Laurel Glen entirely even if I do love him. Evan has to give a little, too. And I'm not sure compromise is in his vocabulary.*

Chapter Nineteen

The bright and cheery morning light streamed into Meg's little kitchen Monday, defying both the weatherman's forecast of April showers and her mood. She stared into her almost empty coffee cup and wondered absently how long the human body could go without proper rest. If she didn't get a good night's sleep soon, she just might find her way into the record books!

The knock at her kitchen door speared her aching head, notching up her annoyance. Opening the door to Evan's smiling face did nothing to calm her flaring temper.

"What do you want?" she asked ungraciously.

Evan grinned and held up an empty cup. "I wondered if I could borrow a few things."

He looked guilelessly hopeful, a lock of iron-gray

hair falling over his forehead. She steeled herself, refusing to feel guilty for being less than enthusiastic about finding her tormentor grinning on her doorstep at ten o'clock in the morning.

"What?" she demanded, not giving an inch.

"Sugar?" he tried.

"Fine... What else?"

Evan blinked and frowned. "Else?"

"You said you wanted to borrow *a few* things. Sugar is only one thing. Unless, of course, you only wanted a few granules, and in that case I doubt you'd need the cup."

He chuckled. "Oh...uh...an egg or two. And maybe a piece of bread or..."

"Two," she finished for him. "Didn't you do any food shopping before you moved in?"

Evan shrugged. "Cris was having a bad day and I didn't want to bother her with directions to stores and the like. Jim had to work."

"I suppose this is to become breakfast."

"That's the plan. French toast. But if it's too much trouble—"

"Oh, just be quiet and go into the parlor. Your breakfast will be ready in a minute," she said, completely surprising both of them. Meg whirled away, stomping to the refrigerator. What was it about a big strong man looking helpless that melted a woman's resolve?

"I don't want to be a bother," he said, stepping in the door to dominate the small space.

She stopped herself just before slamming a carton of eggs onto the counter. Propping a hand on her hip, she turned to him. "Yes, you do, Evan. Your whole purpose in coming to Pennsylvania is to bother me. I don't care what you tell yourself. I don't care what you told my brother or your daughter about us, nor do I care what your agenda is. Now, go into the parlor before you leave wearing these eggs."

Evan gave her one of those silent cowboy nods she knew Jack had learned at his knee. She successfully hid a fond smile by turning away since he was sure to have misinterpreted it had he seen it. Any good feelings were all about Jack.

Now, if she could only convince herself of that!

Us. She'd called them an *us.* Evan grinned and settled into Meg's overstuffed sofa. She might be mad, but Meg had just lost a major battle. The loud clang of a pan being slammed onto the stove resounded through the cottage, bringing Evan back down to earth quickly.

He winced. Maybe this wasn't such a good idea after all. The bang of a cabinet door followed by a loud muttering made him wince. And made him sure he'd blown it again.

When would he ever learn to stick to his plan? He was supposed to run into her accidentally around the farm. Strike up a conversation. Show her how compatible they were. Not knock on her door using a thinly disguised excuse just to look at her.

But he'd gotten to the foreman's cottage by eight o'clock that morning. He'd put all his things away, then looked out the window, knowing she was over here just across the way. He hadn't been able to stop himself from coming over to see her. Just to be with her.

Crash!

Evan winced again. Well, that wasn't exactly the sound of warmth. When would he ever learn?

A few crashes and bangs later she stood in the doorway. "It's ready."

He vaulted to his feet. "Meg, I truly didn't mean to bother you this way. I just wanted to see you."

"Well, finally. A little honesty."

"I haven't been dishonest. A little covert maybe, but no falsehoods. I did have business in the area."

Her only reaction was to arch one of those perfect dark brows of hers in profound disbelief.

"I did!" he protested, but caved in under that blue-fire stare of hers. "My business was with you. Okay! I came to convince you we were made for each other. And that I love you."

"I liked the subterfuge better." She sighed. "Just eat, Evan. I think I've had about all the honesty I can take for now." And with that said, she turned and marched out the back door.

Evan looked at the table—at the French toast she'd made—but he'd lost his appetite. It wasn't that the food didn't look tasty or wasn't beautifully prepared. It was that he'd let her push him into making a declaration she might not have been ready to hear. And one she certainly didn't seem to be in any hurry to return.

Evan's next contact with Meg didn't come until late the next day. He found her sitting on the top rung of a pasture fence staring out across the meadow. The rolling hills were even greener now than when he'd arrived. Temperatures fluctuated from day to day, as did the basics of the weather, but neither did so as wildly as he was used to. Today the rain clouds had blown away by midday, but the ring was too muddy to allow more than the most elementary training.

"Slow day," he said casually, stepping up onto the fence to settle next to her.

"I was able to work with Prometheus. I'm telling you, that big boy is Olympic quality."

"I watched from the window in the stable door. You're a wonderful rider."

She stared over at him, her eyes narrowed. "Thank you. I'm sorry about yesterday. I haven't been sleeping well."

"No. I'm sorry."

"You should be. You're the reason," she said on a deep sigh.

He didn't know how to reply to that. "I don't know if I'm sorry for that one. You're the reason I'm not sleeping too well myself. I missed you after you left. Colorado, I mean. Not your cottage yesterday, though sharing my breakfast with you would have been nice. I really didn't mean for you to have to cook for me."

She shrugged. "I didn't mind."

"Could have fooled me." He chuckled. "And the pots, too. It got pretty noisy there for a while."

"Okay, maybe I did mind. But it was your intrusion into my life that I really minded."

Okay. Now he was starting to lose *his* patience! "Why? Because I make you want things you're afraid to reach out for?"

She stared at him for a long moment. "Did it ever occur to you that I like my life just the way it is?"

"You sound like me not that long ago. I thought my life was perfect, too. Then my son went off on a quest to find you, and my daughter started off on a new life not long after."

"There's the difference between us. I've never said my life is perfect. I said I like it here. Laurel Glen is my home whether I own one square inch of it or not. Exactly what are you offering me?"

"A chance for a life with me. I love you. I want you in my life. To be a part of my life at the Circle A. And Colorado has a lot to offer. You act as if

Jackson and Beth and the kids won't be there. As if Denver isn't a relatively short drive away.''

"What about my life here? My family here?"

"They're Ross's family, Meg. Jackson is your family. I'd like to be."

"Maybe you don't understand. I helped raise those kids. I love them like they are mine. Do you love Jack less than Crystal?"

"Of course not!" he replied, outraged by the suggestion.

"Then why would I love Hope and Cole any less than Jack?"

He shook his head. For that he simply had no answer, nor did he have one for their dilemma. Maybe there wasn't one. He didn't know. But one thing he did know—an Alton could be just as stubborn as a Taggert. He wasn't about to give up, but he could see his pressure was just making her dig in her heels.

So he jumped down and just looked up at her for a moment, sitting there like the queen of all she surveyed. Behind her, clouds had begun to gather beneath the waning sun, setting the stage for the most magnificent sight he'd ever seen.

Beams of light reached down, tingeing the Lord's creation with vivid hues and turning the fluffy clouds a fiery orange-pink. Her blue eyes exactly matched the sky that tried to peek around the clouds. But it was she, not the sky and its glory, who took his breath away. He couldn't lose her, yet he could see that she fit here in her birthplace. How was he to compete with the pull of a lifetime?

"Well, I guess there's no reason we can't still be friends," he said, hoping, praying she'd tell him he was wrong. "Maybe get together for dinner whenever I come east to visit Cris and Jim."

She looked ready to cry. That couldn't be bad, could it? At least, he didn't think so. Then, as he studied her crumbling composure, something occurred to him. She was a beautiful, desirable woman, yet he'd never taken her out on a date. Nevertheless, he'd already told her he loved her and hinted at marriage. What kind of message had that sent? Not a good one, that was for sure.

He'd gotten everything all wrong from the beginning, and since coming to Pennsylvania they'd gotten even more turned around. What had happened to courtship?

Chagrined, Evan stuffed his hands into his back pockets. A romantic he obviously wasn't.

Maybe it was time to make up for that. Maybe he needed to treat her more romantically as well as think romantically himself. Maybe it was time to fix the one thing he could between them.

"So, would you like to have dinner tonight? There's no sense wasting what precious time we have together before I have to leave."

She took a deep breath and straightened her spine

as if working up her resolve. "I'm glad you're willing to be so reasonable about it."

"I can be real reasonable, Meg," he told her, trying to get her to relax in his presence. "So what about dinner?"

She nodded slowly, hesitantly. "All right. Dinner. What time?"

Chapter Twenty

"This is *such* a bad idea," Meg told her reflection as she finished running a brush through her hair.

It was five minutes to seven. Except for the butterflies in her tummy, she was ready. Oh, who was she kidding? She doubted she'd ever really be ready. Not for a date with Evan. And not to let him go, either.

But she was going. She had on her favorite red dress, which usually made her feel upbeat, but it wasn't working. Hard to be as happy as it usually made her feel, because soon she'd have no choice but to let him go if he left for Colorado.

If was a very big word, however, and she was going to have to make good use of it. If she could get him to stay with *her*. If she could show him that traveling with her, sharing her adventures and her life at Laurel Glen would enrich his life, then there would be no goodbye.

And if she failed?

She grimaced and walked away from her dresser. His invitation to dinner and his easy capitulation still stung. When he'd given in so easily, her heart had clenched. Then her practical side had taken over. It wasn't as if he'd be out of her life completely, she'd told herself. They could be friends, loving friends, even if most of the time there would be half a continent between them. And she'd have her memories to sustain her between his visits to Laurel Glen and hers to the Circle A.

So she'd accepted this dinner invitation, because however unsatisfying such a limited relationship would be, she'd tried to tell herself it would be better than nothing. Now she wasn't so sure.

This wasn't like other times she'd met interesting people on her travels, spent time with them, enjoyed good laughs and lighthearted fun, then had gone home with lots of snapshots and fond memories— and no regrets. She'd simply added their names to her Christmas card list and gone on with her life, richer for having known them but no poorer for their absence.

It wasn't like that this time. Because this was Evan. And a limited relationship just might be more painful than even the weeks since returning from Colorado had been. That left her with only one choice, since she didn't want to leave her life behind. Meg had to show him how wonderful and rewarding her life actually was. She had to show him what he could share, and all he'd be missing if he gave up and went home.

His knock on her door wasn't a surprise, but her heartbeat still quickened. She'd decided she had to trust the Lord about her path and the man she'd met along it. Now, if he would only learn to look outside the narrow scope of his own life, he'd see how good and full their life together could be.

She stopped when she reached the door. She could see his shadowed image through the curtains. *"Please, Lord, guide me tonight,"* she whispered, knowing she had no chance on her own.

"Goodness," she gasped when Evan turned to face her with a spring bouquet of lilacs and daffodils in his hands. "Do you treat all your friends like this? If you do, you must have scores of them."

"Only special friends." He handed her the flowers. "So far, only you."

Meg buried her nose in the fragrant petals and inhaled. "Umm. Spring. It can't happen soon enough to suit me." She couldn't help noticing the disappointed look that came over Evan's face and wondered at it. Who on earth didn't like spring? Deciding that train of thought would only sidetrack her from her objective, she asked, "Would you like to come in while I put these in water?"

He nodded, a nod achingly like his son's. Meg was halfway to the kitchen before she realized how easily she thought of him that way now. As Jack's father. And even though she hadn't known she did at the time, she no longer resented him for having the opportunity to be a father to Jack that death had denied Wade.

She felt Evan's presence in the kitchen doorway as she got a white pottery pitcher out of the cupboard. He leaned against the doorjamb with his ankles crossed, watching her, his attention making her hands fumble a bit. She continued to arrange the flowers, trying to ignore him. Finally wondering at his stillness, she glanced over at him and paused. There was a strange look in his eyes and an equally mysterious expression on his face. She was puzzled by that and was compelled to ask, "What is it?"

"You do that so easily. And it actually looks good—not like a bunch of flowers stuffed in a vase but not all stiff and formal, either. Everything seems to come so naturally to you."

"Thank you," she replied, though she didn't have a clue why he was so amazed by her. She was just...her. Shrugging, she dried her hands and took the flowers into the living room to rest on a table that sat beneath the front window.

"There we go. All set. Shall we go?" she suggested, then turned and noticed Evan looking at the series of five pictures that hung on her dining-area wall. "Amelia did that series on the cruise I met her on."

"Are they of a sunset or a sunrise?" he asked, his tone preoccupied.

"A sunset," she told him, walking back to the photos Amelia had given her as a housewarming gift. "Didn't you meet her through Ross?"

"No. I introduced Ross and Amelia. She came here to do a pictorial history of the county and the families of its founding fathers."

"Hmm…" he said, his voice vague once again. "Jackson brought a copy home with him—it was interesting. The colors in these are incredible. What island is that?"

"St. Thomas. It's lovely there."

He continued to stare at the photos, giving her an idea.

"Suppose we go to dinner, and when we get back I'll show you my albums from some of the trips I've taken."

He smiled. "I'd like that. I guess we should go. I hope you don't mind riding in Jim's Mustang. He insisted I borrow it. I think he's convinced I'm in some sort of midlife crisis. Cars mean very little to me usually, but the truth is I wanted one of those babies in the worst way back in '69. Unfortunately, I was too busy trying to afford a new truck."

Meg grinned. "I wanted one, too. I asked for one for graduation. My brother gave me one. Red, just like Jim's." She held up her index finger and thumb. "Except it was three inches long!"

Evan chuckled. "So let's go indulge our fantasies, shall we?"

Three hours later Evan took Meg's key from her hand and, trying to ignore the jolt he felt when their fingers touched, opened her front door. The time had flown by as they shared stories about their homes. Their lives. Her family. His quest to build the Circle A. It had felt to him as if each had been trying to impress the other. And he had to admit, he was impressed.

There was no question that the Taggerts had a long, rich heritage. There had been struggles and victories, tragedies and triumphs in the family's history, and none more compelling than those of the past three generations.

The door swung open and he handed Meg back her key, unsure if the invitation for coffee and some more conversation was still open. On the threshold, he hesitated.

Meg turned after stepping up the one step into the cottage. "Aren't you coming in?"

Not wanting to look like a fumbling boy, he took her hand and stepped closer. The step put them at the same height and he stared into her eyes, then let his gaze drop to her lips. "A dinner date is hardly complete without a good-night kiss, Meg."

"This was a date?" she asked, then smiled shyly. "Yes, I suppose it was."

"Glad to see you agree," he murmured, and leaned forward to cover her lips with his. For the sake of propriety and, to be honest, his sanity he didn't prolong the kiss. He would not consider taking the kinds of liberties Wade Jackson must have, even though she was now a mature woman.

But no one said living a virtuous life was easy. He stepped back, well aware of the effect she had on his mind and body. "Good night, honey. Maybe I'll see you tomorrow."

Her fingers covered her lips for a moment and disappointment flooded her gaze. "Oh, you're leaving? I did so want to show you some of the albums. Just for a little while. I've been so many wonderful places, Evan. I'd love to share them with you."

Put like that, how could he refuse? Evan steeled himself for battle the only way he knew would work. He prayed. *Okay, Lord. Here's where You come in. Keep me from making any wrong moves.*

After a quick deep breath he nodded and followed her inside. He looked around the quaint parlor and chose a chair by the fireplace, hopefully putting a coffee table between them.

"I'll just make us some decaf. Why don't you put some music on."

She left him there, palms sweating, his mind in a turmoil. He should never have kissed her. It sharpened his desperation, reminding him how crucial each moment he spent with her was.

When she returned she set the coffee tray on the low table in front of him and sank cross-legged to the floor facing him. The table next to his chair held a lamp and opened like a cabinet. She pulled out a couple of baskets, each full of small albums that held thirty-five-millimeter photos.

"Would you tell me something?" she asked, tilting her head at a beguiling angle. "Why were you so drawn to the sunset study Amelia did?"

Now, this was embarrassing. He had to answer a world traveler whom he loved but who he was pretty sure saw him as a country bumpkin. But lying would get him nowhere in the long run and it would be wrong besides. He was trying to arrange a future here and he doubted the Lord would reward subterfuge. "I've never seen the ocean, Meg. Until I flew here when Cris was hurt, I'd never been in a plane bigger than an eight-seat commuter."

She didn't seem at all surprised. Perhaps he'd told her when he'd told her about his early life. "Why?" she asked which surprised him.

"I think I told you travel has never interested me. With my past it's only meant worry and uncertainty. Where would I sleep tonight? What would I eat?" He shook his head. "I wouldn't enjoy it."

"I understand how you feel about travel, Evan. But it isn't full of uncertainty if you know you have a home to go to afterward. It's an adventure. It's opening up your mind to new sights, sounds and cultures,'' she explained, her eyes and gestures full of the passion for living he just loved about her.

But still…did she think he was an idiot or so stuck in his ways he couldn't enjoy new experiences? "I know there are things to see that are different from my everyday life. Touring the historical sights of Philadelphia was interesting when Jack and Beth took me. I didn't like the hustle and bustle of the city, but seeing the Liberty Bell, Independence Hall and all the other things from Colonial America was very moving.''

She flipped open a small book she'd pulled from one of the baskets. "So what do you think I felt at Machu Picchu on my trip to the Andes in Peru? Machu Picchu is called the Lost City of the Incas because no one knew it was there until the early twentieth century, and archaeologists still don't know why it was built there on that beautiful spot.''

Evan studied several photos of the terraces and cliffs of the city that had so moved her. Even the pictures conveyed an air of mystery. Meanwhile Meg rooted through the cabinet, then handed him another book. On the front it was marked "Turkey.''

"This is a military cemetery in Gallipoli on the Dardanelles near Istanbul,'' she said, pointing to a picture of row after row of small gravestones. "It has such an air of reverence and pride to it. The incredible thing about it is that the Turks buried a quarter of a million Allied soldiers during World War I as heroes, even though they died invading Turkey.''

Evan found even the photos stirred his emotions, but she wasn't finished. ''And it isn't just feelings, but sights, too.'' She gave him yet another book. ''Here's my album from a trip to France.'' She flipped to a spectacular photo of what looked like a church, with a village surrounding it, built on top of a rocky promontory that rose abruptly out of the sea. It appeared to be an isolated island reflected in exact detail in the water around it. ''This is Mont Saint Michel. It's a monastery. You can see it for miles as you approach it. To get to it there's a causeway that's underwater at high tide.''

She kept going, showing him pictures from Egypt with her on a camel. In India she rode an elephant. A tan Range Rover was her transportation across the Serengeti Plain.

Evan's heart fell. She'd gotten her point across. It *was* an interesting and rewarding way to spend time. And it was the reason she'd become the person she was—the woman he loved. So how was he going to get her to give all that up for him? And if giving up this part of herself would change her, why would he want her to?

She talked about Peruvian ruins and French monasteries the way he did trips into Denver. Somehow he didn't see her being impressed with the chance to go to Antique Row. But he had to keep trying. His love had been enough for Martha, and he had to hope it would be enough for Meg, too.

Chapter Twenty-One

Meg looked up at Evan. His troubled expression wasn't what she'd been trying to achieve. She'd wanted him to see how much fun they could have traveling together. He'd looked interested at first, but now he just looked... Bored? Uncomfortable?

"Well, enough of this," she said, taking the last album off his lap. "I didn't mean to bore you."

He blinked. "I'm not bored in the least. Just feeling a little unsophisticated. I'm the one who must seem pretty boring."

"Don't be silly. I loved your stories about Jack and Crystal growing up and about how you expanded the Circle A."

Evan smiled. "And I enjoyed the tales of the infamous Granny Taggert who lived to such a ripe old age and was still whacking Ross for his language a week before she died."

Meg was relieved. That was better. She reached back into the end table and pulled out a big wide album that took up the whole bottom of the cabinet. "Then you'll really enjoy this. It's full of pictures of Taggert ancestors and starts with a set of eighteenth-century miniatures. And wait till you see the way Jack's resemblance to the family has been around for over a century."

Meg returned from her historical society meeting late the next day as Evan walked out his front door. He was so handsome it sometimes took her aback. If he looked like this in his ranch work clothes, she couldn't wait to see if she could get him into black tie.

She detoured to him, determined to take the next step in her personal campaign to show Evan about life in her world. She spread her arms and gave him a smile as sunny as the day. "Isn't it beautiful?"

He smiled fondly. "Spring's the best. Right?"

She nodded. "I talked to Jack this morning. It's snowing in Colorado. However do you stand winter going on and on this way?"

"Funny, I talked to him, too, and I found myself wishing I was there to see it. I love snow the way we get it. If you'd waited around you'd have seen how fast it melts. Winter comes to the high plains only in visits and goes away quickly till the next time the mood strikes. I guess the respites we get make it less difficult to bear. And then there's the dry air that doesn't make it feel colder or hotter than it really is, the way the humidity does here. I couldn't believe how sticky and uncomfortable eighty-five was when I got here the day Cris was hurt.''

Meg decided there was little she could do to argue with his assessment of local weather, since no one liked the humidity. The only thing it was good for was keeping everyone's complexions from getting too dried out. Somehow saving on the cost of moisturizers as a reason to move his entire life seemed a bit thin. Better to move on to the real objective. Evan in a tux.

''Now that we've discussed the weather, I wondered if I could ask a favor,'' she said.

He raised an eyebrow, and his silver-blue eyes widened in interest. ''Ask away.''

''I've been working on a benefit for the historical society and I have to attend and I thought...'' Meg hesitated. ''I wondered if...'' She grew so nervous her palms began to perspire. She'd never asked a man out before. And at this moment she felt like anything but the modern woman she'd always thought she was.

Evan's expression shifted and he pinned her with one of his probing looks. ''Meg, are you asking me to escort you somewhere?''

''Oh, Evan.'' She laughed to herself, laying a hand on his forearm. ''This is a new experience for me.''

He chuckled, and the sound of his voice tingled along her spine. Oh, she wanted a life with this man.

"Actually, everything I've experienced with you is new to me," he told her, grinning. "I'd be happy to go with you. Is there any particular dress code?"

She grimaced. How would he feel about a formal occasion? "I'm afraid it's black-tie."

"I think I can handle it. Just point me to a good rental shop. Hopefully they can fit me."

"Actually, Cole has more than one tux, and you two are close to the same size. He may be an inch or two taller, but your cowboy boots would make up the difference."

"It wouldn't bother you if I wore them?"

"Are you kidding?" She gave him a smile and a wink. "Those boots are part of the charm, cowboy. The benefit is Friday night. We'd need to leave by seven so I can be there early, since I'm part of the committee."

He gave her one of those short nods and said, "I'm looking forward to it." Then he looked at his watch. "Oh. I have to get a move on. I promised Ross I'd meet with a buyer about that hunter he's brokering for a customer." He chuckled again and shook his head. "A hunter named Hunter. What are people thinking? Anyway, the buyer owns a rental stable and Ross is worried about it being the right place for this horse. He wanted my opinion. While I'm talking to him, Ross is paying a surprise visit to his stable to get an idea of the level of care his animals get.''

She smiled. ''Teamwork. I'm counting on you to make sure Hunter gets a good home. He's a sweetie. Did anyone call you about dinner at Laurel House tomorrow night?''

He nodded. ''I'll be over at Cris and Jim's most of the next several days working on the addition. But don't worry, I'll see Cris sends me home Friday in plenty of time to get myself presentable for your friends.''

A mischievous idea popped into Meg's head and she decided to go with it. It was time he knew how attractive she found him. She bounced up on tiptoe and kissed his cheek. ''Honey,'' she said in a low Mae West sort of tone, ''you're more than presentable with baby spit up on your shoulder and horse manure on your boots. And don't you dare leave the hat home, either.''

Then she whirled away and all but danced to her door. Only then did she turn to see what effect she'd had. And that buoyed her spirits until Friday night. Because Evan stood as if rooted to the spot staring after her. She gave him a jaunty little wave and went the rest of the way inside.

Evan tugged at the cuffs of the jacket, then knocked on Meg's door. Cole's tux fit just fine, but Evan was used to Western cuts with their yoked shoulders and more comfortable fit. He felt as if he were wearing someone else's suit. Which he was, he reminded himself. What really bothered him was that he felt as if he'd stepped into someone else's life. Nothing around him was familiar. Not even the clothes on his back. And the call from Jack on Wednesday had filled him with homesickness. At first he hadn't realized what his mood was all about. But when Meg had brought up the snow he'd realized how much he missed his home.

He knew Meg didn't understand, and he was beginning to despair that she ever would. That she ever could. She moved from place to place so easily. He wished he had her marvelous ability. Maybe it was their childhoods that had spawned the real difference in them, not their adult lives.

She'd had security and family from the first, even if her father hadn't been all he could be. She'd still had this place and her grandmother and brother. It was strange how her life and Jackson's had more than paralleled each other's in that respect. Could the stability of her childhood have been what enabled her by age eighteen to strike out on her own in search of her dreams?

And him? Well, his dream had come true at the same age, but it had been the opposite of what Meg had been searching for. His dream had been of a place to call home. Of a family to love and one that would love him back. Of sleeping in the same bed each and every night of his life.

He honestly didn't see himself managing well away from that.

But then Meg opened the door. And in a flash he knew he could hang on and suffer this emptiness, because she filled it with her very presence. For her he would endure his homesickness. He needed only to hang on until he convinced her that he could give her a good and complete life full of the one thing in life that really mattered.

Love.

"What?" she asked when he'd apparently stared at her for too long.

He grinned, embarrassed by his rudeness. Now that he focused on the brilliant sapphire satin dress, he knew what to say. "You're so beautiful, blue eyes. You amaze me sometimes." This was one of them. "You just always look so perfect."

"I think the accepted coy reply is supposed to be, 'What, this old thing?' but that would be less than truthful. The truth is I shopped my little feet nearly off trying to find the perfect thing to wear for you tonight. So, instead I'll say, Thank you, kind sir." She dropped into a curtsy worthy of the throne rooms of Europe.

"Well, ma'am," he said, tipping his hat, "you more than succeeded." He put out his hand. "Ready?"

"Just let me get my wrap." He watched her go, wondering how she'd found a dress that so perfectly matched her eyes.

Evan realized within moments of their arrival at the historic house where the benefit was being held that Meg was more than just a committee member. She was a vital part of the proceedings. He watched as she greeted arrivals, directed waiters, solved last-minute kitchen problems and soothed the ruffled feathers of an older matron who felt slighted by someone. She was part diplomat, part counselor, part organizer and all woman.

He wanted her to be his woman.

Ross and Amelia, Cole and CJ, and Adam Boyer and Xandra were all in attendance, so he didn't feel abandoned while Meg ran the event practically single-handedly. What he felt was pride. Especially when she acted as MC of the night's white elephant auction and raised a nice piece of change to save a 1700s farmhouse from destruction.

With style, grace and wit she auctioned off everything from dates with eligible singles to concert tickets to a year's worth of riding lessons at Laurel Glen. There were paintings, a record collection and an ugly white elephant, too. The latter was the signature piece of the night. The bidding for the "honor" of keeping it for a year only to return it to be auctioned off the following year was hilarious as Meg urged the bids higher and higher by taunting her friends, neighbors and family. Imagine his surprise when he won the honor.

After the auction was completed, the real entertainment began and Evan was determined to be entertained. The orchestra started playing a romantic slow song and he swept her into his arms. Then he dragged in a breath and with it came her scent, an alluring mix of floral and spice. He swallowed. Holding her was magical. He loved this woman, and prayed he would soon find a way to win her heart.

"This is my favorite piece of music," she whispered, then looked right and left as if checking to see if they'd drawn any attention.

"I think it's going to be my favorite from now on," he admitted, trying to ignore her obvious nervousness. He wished he knew why she'd grown anxious now that she'd joined him when she'd handled the earlier part of the evening with such ease and poise.

"So this isn't too unbearable for you?"

Sometimes he got the idea that she thought he was too rough-and-tumble to be let off a leash. Did she think he was going to break into a Texas two-step at any moment? "No different than one of our formal grange events. We aren't completely uncivilized in Torrence. And I often travel to Denver on business. I eat in real five-star restaurants and stay in top hotels. I learned how to behave in polite company years ago, Meg.''

Her cheeks flamed. ''I'm so sorry. I never meant to imply… I just thought… No, actually I guess I didn't think at all. I wanted you to have a good time tonight. To see that I really do have a life here, in spite of what you seem to think. Your world is just so different from mine.''

He chuckled, trying to put her at ease and sorry he'd said anything. To recapture the moment, he leaned down and kissed her nose. ''Relax. I wasn't offended. I just wanted you to know you could let me roam around unattended among your friends.''

''But I did know that! If I've been nervous it's because I've never brought anyone with me to an event before. Everyone has been staring and asking the most intrusive questions and I have no answers.''

He could imagine their questions. He'd been asking them himself. ''Let them ask! Then smile and say it's none of their business. Or do what Cris would do. Make up an outrageous answer and set them on their ear.''

''Normally, I'd do just that, but this is different. Special.'' She pursed her lips jokingly and stiffened her spine. ''Thank you. I'll do exactly what you suggested from now on!''

''Good girl.'' He grinned. ''Now, I hate to mention this, but the song ended and we're still dancing.''

* * *

The night seemed to fly by after that—a continuous round of chatting, mingling and enough delicious finger foods to pile on a pound or two. Late in the night after the bids and donations had all been tabulated, Meg announced the amount raised and everyone congratulated her as if she'd done it alone. Then he realized she almost had.

He was proud to walk out with Meg under one arm and the elephant under the other. "What are you going to do with that awful thing?" she asked, laughing.

"You mean Jumbo here? Now, that's a good question. He won't exactly go with the decor in my cabin back home, will he? I guess Cris can hold on to it until the historical society needs it next year. She'll have plenty of closets soon."

Meg showed no reaction to the idea of him going home. She just smiled and said, "No. No, I guess it doesn't fit in the Western décor of your cabin."

Chapter Twenty-Two

Cole walked into his exam room with a chart in his hand and a smile on his face. "Crystal! Hello, I just noticed the name," he said, and gave the chart a wave. "We missed you at the white elephant auction last night."

She laughed. "Jim had to work at the last minute. Dad brought his new *pet* over for me to store. It seemed silly for him to take it to Colorado and have to ship it back."

"Ah, yes." Cole chuckled. "The proud white elephant winner. I honestly don't think he meant to bid. And speaking of new pets, who do we have here?" he asked, eyeing the too-thin puppy on the pedestal exam table in the center of the room.

"This is Miracle. Jim showed up with him late last night and we wanted him checked out first thing," she explained.

Cole tilted his head, trying to put a name to the breed. "You've met Dangerous. He looked as bad as this little guy when I found him. I couldn't resist him, either. So where did Miracle come from? And why Miracle?"

"Jim found him last night when he went out to investigate a crime scene."

Cole picked up the pup and looked him over, grinning again at the smell of some flowery shampoo and if he wasn't mistaken cream rinse, too. He chuckled. "Scent to the contrary, he is a male. Breed—"

Crystal jumped in, clearly distraught. "Tell me he isn't part pit bull. Jim didn't think he was, but he's so small, I don't know how he could tell."

"Jim's right. He doesn't have pit skull characteristics. They're unmistakable."

"Oh, good," she breathed. "We've been calling him Miracle because he was in a pen with several fighting dogs and they hadn't torn him apart. The state police broke up a big dogfighting ring and Jim was the investigator called in. He brought Miracle home because he didn't want him destroyed unless it was necessary."

That sobered Cole. "Good for the police. As for this fella, Miracle's very apropos. He was likely destined to be bait for the others to practice on." Cole turned him on his back, pleased that the pup was completely nonaggressive. "I'd say he's some sort of retriever mix. Retrievers are usually great with kids. Are you going to keep him?''

"We talked about sending him to Jackson with Dad because of the construction, but by this morning we decided we'd keep him if you thought he'd be safe with the baby."

Cole nodded and started a thorough exam on the pup. "He'll need shots if we're keeping him in the family, so I may as well get that started, too. So if your father's talking about leaving I guess he's leaving Meg behind, huh?''

"I'm afraid that's what's going to happen. I talked to him a little while ago and he was more discouraged than ever. He doesn't want to leave without her, but...*home* is very important to Dad."

"So my aunt loses out to the Circle A?" Cole asked, annoyed for Meg's sake.

"No. It isn't the Circle A—the ranch operation. It's that the ranch is his home." Cris went on to explain Evan's early life and his attachment to the only secure place he'd ever known. Cole understood what home could mean to someone who hadn't had one or had lost it. "Also, Dad has never gone anywhere. The idea of travel is as foreign to him as the countries Meg goes to all the time," she added.

"They could compromise," Cole said between teeth clenched around the barrel of a syringe as he used an alcohol swab on the pup's hindquarter to prepare for the shot.

Crystal's eyes widened as the puppy scrambled into her arms with a yelp. "You mean spend some time here and some there? They'd get to see us all more often. Maybe Meg could take fewer trips and Dad could give travel a try. I'll talk to him. This could be the answer. I wonder why neither of them have thought of this."

Cole shrugged. "Ever hear that old saying about not seeing the forest for the trees? Lucky we got to talking about this, huh?"

She stared at him in silence for a long moment, then looked down at the puppy. "Maybe he's more of a miracle than we thought. If Jim hadn't found him, we *wouldn't* have talked, would we?"

Cole laughed. Anyone who thought God was just a casual observer walked through life wearing blinders. Since coming to the Lord he'd been constantly amazed by His power.

Evan dismounted Hunter. He and Ross had decided the horse deserved more than the barely passable rental stable the past prospective buyer had owned. So when Cris had mentioned buying a horse for Jim's birthday, Evan immediately had suggested this one. At least he'd done something right lately. Meg had barely batted an eye the night before when he'd mentioned he wouldn't be around to return the elephant for the next auction.

Determined not to start down a slippery slope,

he shook himself loose of gloomy thoughts. He'd learned that his problem with depression couldn't be conquered with medicines alone. Victory came from medication *and* attitude. The doctor's support helped with one, the Lord's with the other.

He turned to Cris. "Hunter's a beauty, honey. I'd go with him," he told his daughter. "He's big and powerful enough for a man Jim's size, but he's gentle and well behaved enough for someone of Jim's limited experience." He studied his daughter. "But you didn't need me to look him over again, especially when I was supposed to be working on your addition today. I was the one who recommended him. Come on. Tell your old dad what's on your mind. It's almost noon and I'm burning daylight."

"Actually, you are, Dad. You and Meg."

Evan flinched. Now he wished he hadn't asked. He also wished he hadn't told the kids about his feelings for Meg. Last thing he wanted was their pity. "I'm pretty sure there's not going to be a 'me and Meg,' honey. We come from different worlds and I can't seem to find a way to convince her to live in mine. Your dad must be pretty uninteresting to a woman who's seen the world."

"What has you thinking like this?"

He led Hunter into the stable toward his stall and she followed. "I'm not having a problem, if that's what you mean. Meg showed me a bunch of picture albums of her travels. She got her point across. And if that didn't, last night did. I'm just a down-home cowhand, honey, and she's a sophisticated society lady, way too cultured for the likes of me.''

The clip-clop of the horse's hooves on the stone center aisle was the only sound for a long moment. ''That doesn't sound like Meg,'' Cris protested. ''Are you sure she wasn't trying to show you how much fun she has traveling?''

That stopped Evan in his tracks. That did seem to be more like what she'd been saying. And it *had* looked interesting. Not quite the quest for a secure place to lay his head, which is how he'd always thought of travel. He'd begun to think he'd enjoy taking trips now and then. But he also knew he'd want to return to someplace familiar, too. So there was still the East versus the West problem.

''Maybe she was just trying to show me that but, much as I love her, I'm not sure I'd be happy here the rest of the time. I'm a cowhand, not a horse-farm foreman. I'm glad to help Ross out and Laurel Glen is a nice place to visit, but it isn't home. I need a purpose in life, honey. I'm too young to retire. Back home I just got involved in a new breeding program with Seth. And as much as I've gone hands-off with the Circle A, I built that place up from a two-bit operation through a lot of hard work, and I love it. Jackson and Beth are there with the twins, too. It's home.''

She crossed her arms, her lips pulled in an angry

line. "What about me? I'm not moving back, Dad. Don't I count at all? Doesn't my baby? Don't you want to be part of our lives, too?"

Evan quickly shooed Hunter into his stall and turned to embrace Cris. "Oh, honey, you know I do. I figured you'd visit and I'll come see you every once and a while."

"Is the office empty, Dad? I think we should talk."

The room used as an office was unoccupied, since it was the foreman's office and at the moment he was as close to a foreman as Laurel Glen had right then. They went in and he sat on the edge of the desk. Cris settled on the old beat-up leather sofa a few feet away. He noticed she'd closed the door when she'd entered after him.

"Now, what's on your mind that's such a secret?"

"You and Meg. Did you ever sit down with her and seriously try to work out a compromise?"

Was he slow or what? "What kind of compromise? She lives here. I live there. There's about seventeen hundred miles between the two."

Cris snorted indelicately and threw up her hands. "You do know what a compromise is, don't you? Maybe you don't. I mean, look at how you handled the problem between Jackson and you with the Circle A. Did it really have to be hands-off? Did it ever occur to you that Jackson would like you as a partner to work side by side with him?"

Evan stared. A huge sense of disquiet descended

on him. Had he blown it with Jackson again? "He never said."

"Because you made it sound as if your mental health demanded you give up working the ranch. He really wanted you to work with him, but he didn't want to put too much pressure on you, so he didn't say anything."

Evan blew out a breath. "I just wanted him to know he'd have as much, if not more, authority at the Circle A as he'd had here."

Cris jumped up and paced to the door. "Like I said—all or nothing. Has traveling with Meg occurred to you at all?"

"I'm not a total idiot. Of course it has. But there's still the east-west problem."

"Could you live here part of the year and at the Circle A the other? That way you'd split yourselves between your children. As your investment counselor, I know you can easily afford it. And Meg isn't exactly penniless. So where's the problem?"

Evan was struck speechless. Could it be that easy? Hard as he thought about it, no reason surfaced why it couldn't work. Maybe it could work. He'd see more of Cris and her baby that way. And Meg loved spring. He could arrange two each and every year for her with the differences in climates. And if they lived three months in each place, he wouldn't get too homesick, especially if he had Meg with him.

He gathered his daughter in his arms and gave her

a bear hug and a big smacking kiss, then put her away from him. "Thank you, baby. You're a genius! Your mama would be so proud of you. She was always one for a compromise."

"And she'd want this for you, Dad. You know that, don't you?"

He nodded. "Oh, yeah. She'd just be annoyed it took so long for me to get to this place in my life. But better late than never. Right?"

Cole, meanwhile, was on his own mission. He didn't intend to propose the compromise, as Crystal planned to do with her father. That would be Evan's place. What he wanted was to make sure Meg was ready to hear what Evan had to say and that she understood how difficult what he was willing to do for her was for him. Which should, of course, show her how much the man loved her.

He owed it to her to make sure she got everything out of life she could. Because Meg had held him together in the worst and darkest days of his life. She'd written to him almost daily when his own out-of-control anger and grief had landed him in a military school far from everything and everyone he'd ever known. She'd guided him. Nurtured him. And finally urged him to come home after years away.

For years he'd credited an instructor for settling him down and later a counselor for telling him to go home. But recently he'd read through all his old letters from Meg, and now he saw that she'd been the one who'd really gotten through to him and kept his love of his home and family alive.

He grinned as he pulled to a stop in front of her Victorian cottage, remembering those first days back at Laurel Glen, when he'd come home and he and Ross had driven her so crazy with their bickering that she'd up and left on a cruise. The cruise had eventually brought Amelia into Ross's life.

The hand of God was on that place and on all of their lives, and now it was time to remind Meg of that and to make sure she understood about Evan. Home to him, because one had been denied him for so long, was as vital as the very breath in his lungs.

Cole found Meg at the back of the cottage. She was up to her elbows in dirt, kneeling in old jeans and gardening clogs, a disreputable old straw hat on her head. "What are you doing?" he asked.

"Getting ready to plant some perennials. I thought vintage roses. Lots of them. An arched trellis there covered in wisteria." Her hands traced a graceful arch. "Maybe honeysuckle around a folly over there." She made a sweeping gesture toward the back of the yard. "And flat trellises for climbing roses on either side of the porch steps."

Cole was surprised at himself. How could they all have forgotten her love of flowers? She'd left so many plants behind in the sunroom at Laurel House. It was a constant reminder of her presence. He pivoted to look at the area where she'd indicated she wanted the folly.

"How about a greenhouse disguised as a folly? Sort of a winter conservatory and sunroom just like you had up at the house?" he suggested.

"My brilliant nephew!" she shouted, and jumped up to hug him.

Ah! The perfect opening, Cole thought.

"I'm so brilliant that I know what this—" he gestured to the dug-up ground and the area that encompassed her plans "—this nesting you're into is all about. Whenever you get stressed you turn to activity. You usually plan a trip. But if you leave this time, your problem would just follow you. It's losing your chance for a life with Evan that has you so churned up." He shot her a grin. "How's that for brilliant?"

Chapter Twenty-Three

Meg just stood there and stared at Cole. He certainly *was* brilliant. Uncomfortably so. She swallowed deeply, getting control of a sudden need to bawl like a baby. Still at sixes and sevens, she turned away and walked back to her digging.

She knelt and concentrated on pulling at a particularly stubborn root for a moment or two. Then she let go, took a deep breath and looked up at Cole. "I know you think I'm wonderful, darling, but apparently I can't replace a chunk of Colorado real estate in Evan's heart. He talks about leaving to go home all the time, even though he said he came here because he loves me. What he came here to do was to talk me into leaving with him so it could be all his way."

"And is that beyond the scope of your love for

him? You go places all the time. Ever wonder exactly why that ranch is so important to him?''

That got her attention. ''Actually, I don't need to wonder, dear. I know. It's the only home Evan's ever had. His parents were worse than abysmal.''

''Crystal told me. In many ways that's how I feel about Laurel Glen, because I couldn't be here for so long.''

She turned and plopped onto her rump in the dirt, pulling up her knees and wrapping her arms around her legs. She frowned, considering her dilemma, but no clear ideas emerged. Her thoughts and emotions were as churned up as her yard. Maybe if she talked it out with Cole she'd finally be able to order her unresolved feelings.

''Pull up a rock, and let's sort this out, shall we?'' she said with a quizzical half smile. Cole perched on the boulder at the corner of the garden and she began. ''First of all, I loved Wade Jackson with all my heart and for more years than he had a chance to live. I loved and valued my work, but I would have given up my dreams for him.''

''That's a powerful statement, considering that the threat of losing this place and everyone here hadn't turned you back from your goal.''

''I loved him,'' she said simply. ''And I loved his child. I gave up Jack so Wade's son would have the kind of life I knew he would have wanted for him.''

''I know you made some painful choices once.

Some great sacrifices. You did it for Hope and me, too.'' Cole gave her a keen-eyed stare. ''But could you do it again?''

Meg nodded decisively. She knew the answer to it all now. ''I could do it again. For Evan. But since meeting him, I've finally seen some of the things that were missing in my relationship with Wade. He was the one who pushed for the intimacy that created Jack. I gave up my principles for him. And then he went back to his helicopter flying. He didn't have a choice by the time he'd met me, but he was frighteningly eager to go just the same. He probably would have gone back if he'd had a choice.''

She let her focus fade as her thoughts turned inward to the relationship she had clung to for so many years. ''Wade had all these medals for valor, you see,'' she continued, thinking aloud now. ''He was a true hero, but he got them by being reckless and that's how he was killed. Earning his last one. He volunteered to go after a downed pilot. His friend later wrote me that his commander had called it a near suicide mission. It turned out it was.''

''So you were angry?'' Cole asked. Again that sharp look, as if he were trying to read her answer in her expression.

She shook her head. ''No. I was too heartbroken and afraid to feel anything else. It was only after meeting Evan that I sat down and really analyzed my relationship with Wade. I still love him. Love doesn't die, you know. And it would be foolish to be angry at a dead young man who'd lacked the maturity to see his own folly. But now I see that it wasn't the perfect relationship I've seen it as all these years. And...and...''

Cole held up his hand, silencing her attempt at deciphering her tangled emotions. "And you don't want to be second to Evan's love of the Circle A, is that it? Jack and Crystal always felt like that and you don't want to feel that way, too."

She smiled, but she knew it was a sad one. "I'm very afraid I would. I've been in that place all my life. To Wade's flying and before that to your father."

"To Dad?"

"I was always second best. Did your grandfather disown Ross for getting Marley pregnant? No. He just helped arrange a wedding. But when I wanted a career he saw as possibly leading to immorality, he turned me out before I'd done a thing wrong."

Cole got up and drew her to her feet. He put his arms around her, then leaned forward and kissed her cheek. "I have more confidence in my aunt Meg than to believe she fell in love with someone who'd put her second to anything on this earth. Evan loves you and he'll put you first. But remember how much the security of the Circle A means to him."

He turned and sauntered away without another word.

Meg picked up her little shovel, then threw it back down. She twisted around and really looked at the churned-up, dug-up yard. Exhausted, she sank to her knees and stared up at the sky.

What if I convinced him to move here? I saw how homesick he is. He's trying so hard, but he can't change who he is, Lord. Or the things he needs—and at this stage of my life, neither can I. And I just can't be near him anymore, knowing I'm going to lose him anyday! I've got to get away from here.

Her decision made, it took all of an hour. A true record for her. She got onto the Internet to her travel club's Web site and found a ten-day Caribbean cruise leaving Norfolk, Virginia, at sunset. It sounded romantic, but she put romance from her mind. It had no place on this trip. She checked to see if she could get a flight, then booked the cruise and flight in a minute or two. She packed swiftly, acting automatically out of long habit. After leaving a message for Ross with his housekeeper, she headed for the airport. She had five hours to make the ship. Talk about perfect timing.

Though resigned and miserable, she was on the move. At least now she was in familiar territory.

Evan begged off working at Cris and Jim's and went right to see Meg. But her car was gone. He smiled when he walked around the side of the house. Her yard looked as if it had been attacked by a demented gopher. A herd of demented gophers, actually. Her shovels and rakes still littered the yard. She must be out buying plants, he decided, and headed home.

When she hadn't returned by dark, he called Laurel House to see if anyone there had seen her.

Ross answered. ''You're…ah…you're looking for Meg?'' he asked, sounding more than a little hesitant.

Evan felt his stomach flip. ''Ross, is something wrong with her?''

''Actually, Evan…I'm sorry to have to tell you this. She left a message with Sally several hours ago, but I only just got it. She's taken off to… Let's see where this time.'' He heard the rustling of paper. ''Carousel Cruise Lines out of Norfolk. The *Destiny*. Headed for the Caribbean. Listen. Don't take this the wrong way, because all of us have driven her to this before. Apparently Meg told CJ that she bugs out like this so no one has the chance to leave her before she leaves them. And Cole had a long talk with her earlier today. It seems as though she feels she's always come second with everyone.''

Evan felt his anger at all of them flare. ''And she hasn't?'' he asked, letting sarcasm show his anger.

Ross sighed. ''Well, actually, she probably has. Definitely did with my father, but as I told you, I tried to make up for that. Anyway, that's where you come in.''

Evan's heart sank. Why hadn't he seen it when

he'd seen the rest? "She thinks she's second to the ranch, too. Right?"

"I'm afraid so. Is there any way you can let her know that isn't true?" Ross sounded hopeful.

"I'd been about to propose a compromise, but now I don't think that'll do it." Was that the end of it? he wondered with a heavy heart.

No. What was he thinking? He loved her and he was no quitter. And he wouldn't quit on his love for Meg. She'd left rather than have him leave her. Wade Jackson had left. Her father had left in his own way. Forget Cris's compromise. Meg would be first with him for the rest of their lives. He'd prove it to her every day.

He'd have to start now, though, so he ended the conversation quickly. "Thanks, Ross. I'll keep you posted."

Trip planning was out of his ken so he called Cris. Jim Dillon was at Cris and Jim's working on the addition, and he had a few ideas, too. Together they constructed a bold plan.

He'd be waiting when Meg arrived in St. Thomas. She wasn't getting away this easily. And if his plans worked, they'd have a three-day honeymoon on the way back to the States. It didn't escape his notice that a man who'd never even seen the ocean was about to trek across it in a quest to win his lady fair.

A few days later, as the plane swooped down to St. Thomas airport, Evan felt his hair stand on end.

The sea sparkled a little too close below and a mountain loomed up to meet them. He wasn't sure how often he could travel if being scared out of his wits was part of all Meg's adventures.

Meg stood on her little balcony and watched as St. Thomas rose on the horizon just after the sun had. It looked like a jewel in the middle of a sea of blue.

And she couldn't care less.

She *did* love the little island—the bustling waterfront and the streets filled with incredible shops. But Evan was back at Laurel Glen or in Colorado. The problem with the island, she'd decided yesterday, was that he wasn't there.

The past days hadn't been the respite she'd sought, but they might have been the most important of her life. She'd learned something vital. She needed Evan at her side.

She gazed out at the harbor as it came into view. The colorful buildings of the bustling port city didn't lift her heart this time. Nothing was as bright now. Nothing was as joyous. Nothing mattered.

Nothing but booking the first flight home and telling Evan she'd live in a tepee at the Circle A if that was what he needed. She could still travel. She'd traveled alone for years. But now she'd have Evan to go home to. And they'd be sure to visit Laurel Glen sometimes. Crystal and her family would surely make Evan want to travel at least as far as Pennsylvania.

She sighed. But all this speculation hinged on one question. Was she too late? It hadn't escaped her notice that he'd freely told her he loved her and that she had never reciprocated—too afraid at first to put her trust in a man, then too stubborn to concede her lifestyle to his.

What if he'd simply tired of pursuit without hope? She prayed he hadn't. She should have seen it before, but old hurts she'd never even tried to deal with had blinded her to the truth. It wasn't fair to Evan to make him suffer because her father hadn't been all he could have been.

Evan couldn't help loving his home or needing the security of living there. She'd been given security and more love in the formative years of her life than he had. Now it was time to give to Evan rather than expect to collect on the old debt of two other men who'd disappointed her.

As the island drew closer, Meg went back into her cabin to lie down. She'd pack after they docked and then head to the airport.

Exhausted, having gotten up much too early, she slept until a knock on her door woke her. She started awake. ''Yes?'' she called, but couldn't decipher the reply. Still fully dressed, she went to answer the door. Her peephole revealed flowers.

"Who on earth would send me flowers?" she wondered aloud, and opened the door.

Her answer stood on her threshold. And it was the last one she'd ever have expected. Shock and joy coursed through her like a sparkling fountain.

"Evan?"

He grinned, completely unrepentant for the shock he'd given her. "Hello, love," he said. "You forgot something?" He handed her the flowers. Lilacs and daffodils—exactly the same as he'd brought her before.

Her brain simply refused to function. She couldn't believe what stood before her. "What are you doing here?"

"You forgot something besides your flowers. Me. I know you're used to traveling alone—but on your honeymoon? I like the ocean, by the way. I'd prefer it a little farther away from the airplane when I'm landing, but I like it."

"Evan, what on earth are you talking about?"

He looked over her shoulder. "The captain says you have an outside cabin with a balcony. Let's go talk out there."

She backed in, afraid to take her eyes off him for fear of waking from this wonderful dream. The feel of the lounge chair under her and the salt breeze on her skin nearly convinced her she was awake. But then Evan tossed a large flat box that she hadn't no-

ticed before onto the other lounge chair and dropped
to one knee in front of her. He was holding a ring.

"I love you, Meg. I'm sorry you thought I loved
the Circle A more. I don't. We'll live in Pennsylvania. In the cottage at Laurel Glen, if you want. And
this will only be our first of many trips together. I
promise. Will you marry me?"

"Okay, now I know this is a dream," she said
shakily, her heart thrumming with a joy she was still
afraid to trust.

He cupped her cheek and kissed her. "Wake up,
Sleeping Beauty," he whispered against her lips. "It
isn't a dream, blue eyes." He pulled back, tilted his
head a bit, a vertical concentration line appearing between his eyebrows. "And I'm afraid I'm no
prince."

"Evan, I can't make you give up that ranch. I love
you too much to take you away from your home. I'll
marry you, but only if we live at the Circle A."

Evan slid the flowers to the deck, removed the box
from the lounge across from hers and sat down. He
stared at her for a prolonged moment. Then he gave
her that heart-stopping lopsided grin. "You're driving me around the bend, woman. You skipped out
about an hour before I went to see you. To propose
a compromise. I guess we'll see if that works."

Meg went still and Evan's grin vanished. "A compromise?" she asked carefully.

The grin was back. "Supposing we plan to split

our time between the Circle A, Laurel Glen and traveling.''

''You'd do that?''

''I'm here, aren't I?'' he asked.

She blinked back a rush of tears. ''I'm beginning to think you really are.''

''Is that a yes? Because I'm not risking these old knees again if you're going to go tossing up another hurdle for me to get over.''

''No hurdles. And don't get up.'' She scooted closer and reached out to him with her left hand.

He held it, but looked searchingly into her eyes. ''I didn't exactly finish my proposal. Will you marry me? Now?''

Meg blinked. ''Now? Like soon? Of course. We're too old for a protracted engagement,'' she said with a smile. ''When do you think we could arrange it?''

Evan grimaced a little and checked his watch. ''It's eight. How about in two hours?'' He turned away and picked up the box she'd forgotten all about. ''CJ says, 'Turnabout is fair play.'''

Meg took the box and opened it. A white lace dress sat nestled in tissue paper. ''I bought her wedding dress,'' Meg said, tears in her voice. ''Evan, we can't just get married. There are legalities.''

He handed her an envelope. ''Taken care of. You left a copy of your birth certificate in the safe at Laurel Glen. Holly Dillon knows someone in the government here who pulled some strings. And Pastor

Jim found us a Christian minister to perform the ceremony. For the rest, Cris found a company that works with this cruise line to arrange weddings on board. We're not the first to do this, apparently.''

She tore the envelope open and found an official-looking marriage license that lacked only signatures.

Meg beamed a misty smile at him. "I don't know what to say."

"Could I suggest yes? I really need to let the captain know the wedding's on. Oh, and the bridal suite just happened to be empty, so I booked it for the return trip. Ross and Amelia are arranging a reception for us when we get home and Jackson and Beth are flying in for it."

It was all so perfect it took her breath away. He had done this for her. They all had. "I guess I'd better get ready."

"Guess you'd better," he said, and gave her one of those quick nods. Her heart turned over as she felt the ring slide onto her finger.

She looked down at it. A single sapphire surrounded by diamonds winked up at her. Until then she hadn't noticed. She'd seen only Evan.

"The captain will come by to escort you to the deck," he whispered in her ear, and then he kissed her cheek and melted away. "Yahoo!" she heard him shout after the cabin door shut behind him.

She laughed. "My cowboy."

* * *

Two hours later on the top deck of the ship called *Destiny,* with the clear blue ocean surrounding them and the sun shining down, Evan Alton and Meg Taggert made solemn promises to each other joining their lives. It might be the autumn of their lives, but they both felt younger than springtime!

Dear Reader,

My, but these two were troublesome. Which was quite a surprise since I've been eager to do Meg and Evan's story for quite a while. It is one of the most requested books I've ever written, but who knew going in just what trouble they'd give me!

Then, as they took on life in the pages, I realized that with all the conflict these two had with each other and with all they had in common, their main problem was as simple and complex as East meets West. How and where it occurs depends on point of view. I also realized that I'd had to wait this long to give them their story. Even three years ago they wouldn't have been able to move on to the life the Lord had for them. Evan couldn't have left the Circle A behind half the year, and Meg still had too much binding her to Laurel Glen until both Hope and Cole were settled. As usual, His perfect timing was at work, and I never even realized it!

And isn't it funny that His perfect timing is the underlying theme of the book?

Watch for His hand in your lives. It's there every day. I find it awe inspiring to look for it and find it so consistently. And you will find it because He is constant.

I love hearing from my readers at: kate_welsh@earthlink.net, but I regret I can only answer e-mail correspondence and letters that are accompanied by a stamped self-addressed envelope when you write through Love Inspired.

Love and blessings,

Kate Welsh

Love Inspired

EVERLASTING LOVE

BY

VALERIE HANSEN

Camp director James Harris reluctantly agreed to let animal therapist Megan White test her program with his troubled kids. But when Megan's young sister and one of the teens disappeared, all James's doubts and anger rose to the surface, and he railed at heaven. Would Megan's strong faith be able to help James regain his…and win his heart?

Don't miss

EVERLASTING LOVE
On sale September 2004
Available at your favorite retail outlet.